SOMETHING OF NOTE

A SWEET SECOND CHANCE ROMANCE

SHOPPING FOR LOVE IN CATALUMA

JEANINE LAUREN

ISBN 978-1-7388343-4-1

AUTHOR'S NOTE

Welcome.

Thanks for visiting the small town of Cataluma, California, a place my friends and I are excited to share with you.

Here in Cataluma, the business owners, are busy getting ready for the event of the year. Are you ready? Turn the page to discover what's happening at the local music store.

If you'd like to know when my next books are coming out, head over to my website (www.jeaninelauren.com) and join my newsletter.

Something of Note is one story set in the Shopping for Love in Cataluma World

Other Sweet Cataluma titles include:

Inking the Deal by Roxie Clarke (Sweet Cataluma), and,

Entangled in Love by Katrina Litwin (Sweet Cataluma)

*E*ugene Baxter came in from the camper van in his friend Pete's backyard and accepted a beer from Madison, Pete's wife.

"Thanks for staying the extra day, Gene," Madison said. "It means a lot that you're here to celebrate his birthday."

Gene looked around the room at the two-dozen people laughing and enjoying themselves. "Not sure he would notice with all these people, but thanks."

"How are you doing?" asked Madison, pulling him into a corner of the kitchen away from others. "I worry about you. You should settle down."

"Can't. Pete got the last good one."

"You are so ridiculous. I liked Chelsea. What was wrong with her?"

"Nothing."

"You both board, like to travel, and have a nomadic lifestyle."

"I know. But it wasn't quite right. Besides, she's with that billionaire boyfriend now, so it turned out okay for her."

"That's my boy," joked Pete, as he broke into their conversation. "Always leave them better off than they started." He shook Gene's hand. "It's good you stayed. Been—what? Ten years since you last helped me celebrate a birthday? We were in Peru."

Eugene winced. He'd tried to forget that trip. "I couldn't let your forty-fifth go un-marked, could I?"

"That's true, isn't it?" said Madison.

"What's true, hon?"

"Gene always leaves women better off than when they met him. I mean, Chelsea's with a billionaire." She counted off Gene's rela-tionships on her fingers. "Sue got a great job with that client you introduced her to…"

Pete reached over and clinked his beer bottle with Eugene's. "Mads is right. Cyn-thia is married to that great guy who has the llama farm in Peru."

Eugene winced again. It had taken a long time for him to get over Cynthia, but from what he knew, she and Arthur were happy, and it was his own fault since he was the one who'd introduced them. Still. He wished he could find a relationship that would stick.

Pete and Madison continued down the path of Eugene's heartbreaks. "Another one sings in Vegas," Pete said.

"Yep. Helped her get discovered," said Eugene, taking another swig of his beer.

"Then there's that one you convinced to finish school," said Madison, "and she left to go to graduate school, didn't she?"

"Oxford. As far away as she could get," said Eugene cheerfully. If he couldn't stop them, he may as well join in and keep the whole conversation light. "It's my lot in life to be the guy who helps them figure out what they want, and then they're gone."

"At least you had fun along the way," said Pete.

"And I still get to keep my nomadic life."

"Where are you heading tomorrow?" asked Madison.

"Should get as far as Oregon by nightfall. Then down to Cataluma. I haven't seen Jock since Christmas, and I feel like I'm neglecting him."

"Jock?" asked Madison.

"My stepfather."

"The man who raised him," said Pete quietly.

"Yes, Madison, even my mother left me," joked Eugene. "Her excuse was the best yet because she died when I was twelve."

"And your father? The biological one?"

"Never met him. He was in the navy. Never made it back."

"I'm sorry."

"It's the way life is, Mads. None of us get out alive."

The mood was solemn for a moment until Pete said, "Hey, there's someone I want you to meet." He steered Gene toward an attractive redhead on the other side of the room. "She's single. Maybe she can be your next project."

"Are you ever going to stop trying to fix me up?" Eugene muttered.

"You're forty-four, Gene. Time to settle down. I will stop once you find one to stick with. There you are, Tracy," he said more loudly. "Let me introduce you to my friend Gene."

Eugene glared at his friend a moment before turning toward the woman and summoning his most charming smile. "Nice to meet you, Tracy."

∾

The next morning, Eugene hooked his custom-made guitar case onto his Ducati SuperSport and finished packing his other belongings into the saddlebag before walking into Pete's house to say goodbye.

"Wish you could stay a few more days. How come you're going so early?" Pete asked, wincing as he took a sip of coffee. Eugene was happy that, unlike the birthday boy, he had stopped at two drinks. "I thought the construction job in LA didn't start for another month."

"I want to give Jock a hand with the Strawberry Festival."

"Strawberry Festival?"

"It's an annual thing in Cataluma. I haven't helped in a few years but, in the past, I've gotten his music students ready to perform. It increases the numbers at the show, advertises his business, builds up Jock's student numbers for the summer. That kind of thing."

"And what about your music?"

"I've got a couple of friends who play on the festival circuit. They're missing a bass player, and I said I'd stand in for a few months."

"Hammer slinger by day, music slayer by night."

"Something like that."

"So we'll see you back in Colorado when? November?"

"That's my plan. I'll be back in the fall to teach my snowboarding students again."

"You should think about getting a consistent job, you know. Maybe a place to call home."

"But that would mean I would need to grow up." He drew a glass of water from the tap, drank it, and then turned to give his friend a quick hug. "And we wouldn't want that."

"See you soon," said Pete.

"Leaving so early?" A bleary-eyed Madison stepped into the room.

"Want to get an early start before traffic gets too bad," said Eugene, giving her a quick kiss on the cheek and a hug goodbye.

Then he walked outside to mount his bike and start the long trek toward the I-5. He needed to get as far as he could today. He was worried about Jock. Though he had called several times over the past few days, he had yet to get a reply. Not even a text. It wasn't like Jock not to answer his calls.

～

Two days later, Eugene parked his bike in the dark parking lot behind Making Sweet Music and knocked on the back door of the store. Jock still hadn't answered his phone, and every time Eugene rang, it went straight to a full voicemail box. Maybe he'd lost his phone and hadn't canceled the number yet. Or maybe something was wrong.

Gene knocked again, harder this time, listening for footsteps and waiting for the back light to be turned on. Nothing. Considering it was only eight o'clock, this was not a good sign. Where was he going to stay tonight?

He mounted his Ducati again and rode over to the local Cataluma Inn. Maybe Aaron would know where Jock was. And where he could pick up a key.

The inn was a nice place that overlooked the river in the south part of town. He parked his bike alongside two others, grabbed his saddlebags and guitar, and walked inside. There at the desk was his old friend, Aaron.

"Look what the wind blew in," said Aaron. He came around to welcome Eugene. "I haven't seen you in how long? Four years?"

"Five," mumbled Eugene, ashamed that he hadn't been around for so long.

"You here to help Jock?"

"Yeah. You know where I can find him?"

His friend looked at him closely. "Um, he's at the hospital."

"What?"

"I thought Sandy would have told you."

"Haven't heard from her," said Eugene. "Why is Jock in the hospital?"

"He was putting up a display of guitars, hanging one from the ceiling, and he fell. Broke a hip. Been swearing a blue streak for several days, apparently. Just wants to get back to work. He'll be glad you're here. Sandy cannot do all of it herself and keep visiting him for instructions every night. The man is worse than a bear that awoke hungry."

"Do you know where Sandy is? I need to get a key from her."

"She's probably home by now. Do you know where she lives?"

"I think so. Just down on Gold Rush Lane?"

"That's the place." If it doesn't work out and you need a place to crash, come on back. We have a few extra rooms tonight."

"Will do. I may be back for dinner anyway. What time does the restaurant close?"

"The pub serves until ten."

"You still have those portobello mushroom burgers?"

"Oh yeah. They're a fan favorite."

"Sounds great. I'll be back in a few."

~

When he got to Sandy's place, she greeted him warmly. Sandy had been Jock's right-hand person at the store for as long as Eugene could remember. She and her husband, Blake, had been there to help Jock after Eugene's mother died, and she had always been a surrogate aunt to Eugene.

"I would have called, but I couldn't find your number or his cell phone."

"Probably in a drawer somewhere," said Eugene. "He never seems to have it with him."

"Interferes with customer service," she said, handing him the key. "He's okay, nothing critical. Just recovering from a hip fracture and a broken arm, but they are keeping him in longer. He'd like it if you could drive over to see him tomorrow, though."

"I'll do that," said Eugene. "And, Sandy, I'll be staying a while so I can lighten your load. Let me know what I can do to help."

"It would be great if you could take over some of Jock's classes. I've had to cancel them for the last week. If we don't finish them, we'll have to refund the money."

"Consider it done," said Eugene. "I'll come down to the store first thing and you can show me the schedule."

"Thank you, Eugene." Sandy reached up to give him a hug, and Eugene bent to meet her halfway. The woman was tinier than he remembered.

"I just wish I'd known earlier. I could have been here a week ago."

"Well, you're here now," she said, stepping back and patting him on the arm. "And that's what's important."

CHAPTER 2

*H*onoria Hudson hoisted her saxophone into the trunk of her bright-red Mini Cooper and slammed it shut.

"You have everything?" asked Bethany, her best friend.

"Yes." Honoria walked around to the driver's side of the car, hugged her friend tight, and handed her the keys to Bethany's basement suite. "Thank you so much for everything. I don't know what I would have done if you hadn't been here."

"It's been great having you," Bethany said. "We haven't spent so much time together since we were in college. And I'm sure our next tenant won't be half as good with the kids. I'm not sure what I would have done without you living here for the past year. You helped me so much."

"We'll have to make sure we don't wait another twenty years before the next good, long visit."

"No. In fact, we should plan a camping trip or—"

"Or a five-star hotel?" said Honoria.

"That is more to your taste, for sure."

"I can't help it if I like creature comforts."

Bethany laughed. "Well, I'm sure you'll be back on top again soon. You always have a way of landing on your feet."

"I hope you're right," said Honoria. She opened the car door, determined not to let the tears fall—at least not until she was out of Beth's sight.

"Once the divorce goes through and he buys you out of the condo, you'll have enough to start again."

"I know. I just wish Crispin would stop dragging things out." She swallowed hard. "It's been eight months since he moved that… that woman into my home," said Honoria. "Meanwhile, Uncle Jock needs my help, so I should get going. I have a long drive, and you know how my mother is. She's mad she can't just up and leave Sunshine Bay to help her brother right now. So she'll hound me until I get to Cataluma and give her an update after I've seen him for myself."

Bethany gave her another hug and stepped back when they heard barking. "Yes, we'll miss you too!" Bethany nodded to the red sable Pomeranian that was still barking from the back seat of the car.

"Shush, Duke," said Honoria. The dog stopped, turned in circles a few times, and lay down.

"He looks ready to go," Bethany said.

"Yes, it seems so." Honoria climbed into the car and rolled down the driver's-side window. "I'll text you when I get to Cali."

"Surely the idiot will have to buy you out of the condo soon."

"Eventually. But meanwhile they are there, I'm without a home, and there's not much I can do about it."

"Well, at least you're free to help your uncle. He'll be relieved to see you."

"Yes," Nora said, putting the car into reverse. "At least there's that. See you soon."

CHAPTER 3

*E*ugene drove to the hospital in Santa Barbara as soon as he woke up the next morning. He found Jock lying in bed, his skin as gray as his hair.

"Dad?"

Jock's eyes fluttered open. "Gene?" His face broke into a smile.

"What happened?"

"Had a tussle with the floor. Floor won."

"What were you doing on a ladder that wasn't high enough for the job?"

"Stupid fool thing to do, and Sandy's already told me off enough."

"How's your hip?

"Hurts like the devil, but apparently it only gets better from here. They're making me exercise it. I was up yesterday walking."

"When can you come home?"

"Probably next week. I got an infection, and they want to make sure I'm okay. Feel like one of those amoebas we had to study in science class under a microscope. Watched for every sign of change or life. They probably think I'll sue or something. I just want to get back to my store."

"Why didn't you tell me you were here? You shouldn't have gone through this alone."

"I wasn't alone. I had company."

"Yeah? Who?"

"People. Don't fuss."

"And when you get out, we'll need to find a place with no stairs."

"Sandy's helping me. We've got that covered. Don't worry. Go down to LA."

"No, Dad."

Jock looked up at him, surprised. "What?"

"Let me help you."

"I don't need a nurse."

"No, but you're going to need some help at the store."

"Doris is coming, or…?" Jock looked confused, as though trying to remember a conversation he'd only half paid attention to.

"Doesn't your sister have her own store to worry about? And, between coming here every night and keeping things together at the store, Sandy's run right off her feet. She looks exhausted."

Jock's face fell. "She looks tired, you say? She never said anything."

"You know Sandy. Never wants to be a burden on anyone. Always there to help."

"Well, Doris made me a promise, and she's a woman of her word."

"What exactly did she say?"

Jock thought for a moment, and then his eyes lit up. "I remember now. She said she'd send one of her kids, but they haven't arrived yet."

"Which one?"

"Probably Robert. Nora's living in Seattle, working for some big dealership her husband's family owns."

"Robert? You mean Bobby? He's just a kid."

Jock glared at him out of the corner of his eye. "If you visited more often, you would know that Rob is thirty-eight years old. He practically runs the store in Sunshine Bay. Doris plans to retire and hand the reins over to him next year."

"But how is he with kids? At least Nora was good with the kids when she helped with some of the festivals back in the day."

"He has one of his own, so he can't be that bad."

"Has a kid of his own?" Eugene had heard something about Bobby getting married a few years earlier. Went to Vegas or Thailand or some place for a destination wedding when Eugene was traveling in South

America. But that was years ago. "How old's the kid?"

"Must be nearly ten now. Rob's been raising Zack on his own since his wife died. On second thought, maybe Doris won't send Bobby. I don't know. She promised she would send someone, though. Then she'll come herself later. She said she'd do it, so she will."

"Rob's wife died? Why didn't I know this?"

"Four years ago. Cancer. Horrible thing. You were in Colorado, teaching. Going through something yourself at the time, I think."

"Probably." He pretended not to remember, but it must have been when he and Lisa had stopped seeing each other. Lisa had left to pursue her dream job, collecting plant samples in the Amazon, with a botanist they'd met while snowboarding. Pete was right: he had rough luck in the relationship department. He glanced around the room at the white walls, the equipment, and the intravenous in Jock's arm. "Look, I'm staying on to help as long as it takes. If Doris sends someone to help, great. If not, don't worry about it."

"No. You've got a job to go to."

"Don't fight me on this, Dad. I'm a damned sight better at fighting than a floor, and look what happened there."

Jock smiled at that. "But what about the job? You go there every year. Won't you be putting it at risk?"

"I'll let them know I'm coming late. After the festival is over will be soon enough. By then, hopefully your summer staff will be back, and..." He looked at Jock's hip. "And we'll have a plan for the next few months figured out."

"Okay. I can't say it doesn't make me feel better knowing you'll be here to look after things while I'm mending. If one of Doris's kids does come, I've told Sandy to give them my room. I won't be able to do the stairs for a few weeks anyway."

"Will do." He gave Jock what he hoped was a reassuring smile. Though Jock seemed to think he'd be navigating stairs in a few weeks, it didn't look promising. "Meanwhile, I'll look for a place for you to stay when you get out that doesn't need stairs."

"Sandy has it all under control," Jock said gruffly.

"What you'd do without Sandy, I'll never know," said Eugene.

Jock blinked at him for a moment. "You know what? I don't know what I'd do without her either."

The nurse came in, wheeling the blood pressure machine, and interrupted their conversation.

"I'll get out of your hair and see what I can do to help Sandy."

Jock grabbed his arm as Eugene leaned over to give him a quick hug. "Thanks for coming, son," he said. "I'm mighty glad to see you."

"I'm glad to see you too," said Eugene, squeezing Jock's good arm. "Get better soon, okay?"

"Oh, and Gene?"

"Yes?"

"Can you check in about the band that's supposed to come? It's a tribute band. Name's in the office. Sandy will find it. I tried to reconfirm with them, but then"—he waved at his torso area—"this happened. I just want to be sure they're coming."

"Sure, I can do that." Eugene stepped out of the way of the nurse, waved goodbye from the door, and headed to his bike, shaken by what he had just seen. Jock. The man who had been there for him since he was eight, always strong, always patient, and always understanding, even when Eugene was going through the teen angst that lasted well into his twenties. Jock needed him, and Eugene was determined to rearrange his life for as long as it took to help his stepfather.

Just as Jock had done for him when he'd needed him most.

CHAPTER 4

*H*onoria parked her Mini behind Making Sweet Music and walked around to let Duke out of the back seat.

"Hey, boy, we're finally here," she said, clicking his lead to his collar. "Let's go for a bit of a walk, shall we?" She locked the car and walked down the street to give the dog time to do his business. She wanted to get acquainted with the little town again. It was only April, but already there were far more blooms than in Seattle. It was also drier, which she appreciated whenever she visited California. Though Seattle had been pretty good to her for the past twenty years, and she had built herself a great career there as an accountant, it was nice to get away from all the reminders of Crispin.

Crispin, or at least things that evoked memories of him, seemed to be every-where. It was like that old Vera Lynn song that her grandmother had played over and over after her grandfather died: *I'll be seeing you in all the old familiar places…* The lyrics ran through her mind whenever she walked down streets they'd frequented, past familiar restaurants, their local gym, and the hospital where she had undergone fertility testing.

Crispin had never seemed to get time off to come with her when she'd visited Cataluma, so it was hers alone. The only men she ever thought of when she was here were her Uncle Jock and his son, Eugene—

the object of her first schoolgirl crush years earlier.

She had finally gotten hold of Jock the previous evening after a kind nurse had walked down the hallway to give Jock the phone. He had barked out instructions as though he were waiting with a list. The first instruction was to see Sandy when she got to town. Sandy would tell her what needed doing, give her a key, and make sure she did things right.

It wasn't clear what Uncle Jock would do without Sandy. Honoria just hoped his newfound grumpiness didn't drive the poor woman away. Even a woman as saintly as Sandy was bound to have a breaking point.

Honoria picked up the little dog's deposit with a small bag and placed the bag into the nearby trash can before picking up her little companion and pushing open the front door of the store.

The tinkle of the bell caused an older woman behind the cash register to look up. When she saw Honoria, the tiny woman's face split in two with the warmest smile Honoria had seen in months. She stepped forward and stooped to hug Sandy with one arm while keeping a tight grip on the wriggling Duke with the other.

"I'm so glad to see you, honey," said Sandy when she stepped back to look up at Honoria. "And who is this?" She nodded toward the little dog.

"Duke Ellington," said Honoria.

"Greatest jazz player of all time. Sandy reached up and patted Duke's head. "A fitting name for your pal. Where are you parked?"

"Out the back. I should bring in my sax and stuff sooner than later. I know you rarely have crime here, but with the way my life has been heading this year…"

"I was so sorry to hear about your breakup," said Sandy. "But you know, it's better to find out now than to wait another decade first."

"I suppose. I just wish I'd known when I was thirty-two and not forty. It has messed with my entire life plan." Honoria laughed.

"Plans change. And sometimes something better comes along when you least expect it." Sandy walked around to the cash register again and pressed a button to open the money tray. She fished out a key and handed it to Honoria. "Here you go, hon. Put your things away, then come on back down and we'll have a cup of tea and a coze. You can use your uncle's room this year. I've made up the bed and tidied it up in there. He won't be able to climb those stairs for several months yet.

"Is it that bad, then? "

"He's a daft old twit," said Sandy. "Why he climbed up a ladder that was too short, I do not know. At least he's getting looked after where he is, and there's no chance of him coming back here anytime soon."

"He must be so frustrated."

"Angry as a wet cat. But there's not much he'll be able to do about it, so I told him he may as well just let us help him."

"Exactly," said Honoria. She set the wriggling dog down on the floor and held his lead so he couldn't go far. The last thing she needed was for Duke to leave his mark somewhere in the store.

"Do you want me to watch Duke for you while you're unpacking?"

"Would you? I can come and get him when I'm done and let him get to know his new home."

She handed the lead to Sandy and left Duke looking between them. He barked a little in protest, but Sandy reached into her pocket and squatted in front of him to hand him a treat. When Honoria left the store, his whole backside was wiggling in gratitude as he looked up hopefully at Sandy again.

Honoria shook her head as she walked back to the car. Was there anything Sandy wasn't prepared for? Who carried dog treats in their pocket? Sandy, of course. The woman was a gem.

CHAPTER 5

*H*onoria had just finished lugging the last of her luggage up the stairs to her uncle's room when the door to the spare room opened and a man stepped out, wearing nothing but a towel. She gasped, stepped back, and averted her eyes, though not before noticing his nearly naked form.

"Who are you?" they asked at the same time.

"I'm Uncle Jock's niece. I'm staying in his room," she said, pointing toward the bedroom.

"Uncle Jock?" he said. "Does that mean you're Nora?" He was looking her up and down as though trying to place her.

She narrowed her eyes at him, and then her eyebrows rose in surprise. "Geno?"

"No one's called me that in years," he said.

"I haven't seen you in years," she said.

"That's true. You must have been—what? Fifteen? And I was expecting Robert."

"He can't leave the store this time of year. I came to help Sandy while Jock's in hospital."

"And you're staying here?" He pointed to her uncle's room. "With me?"

She turned back and looked at him again, her face turning red as she glanced from his eyes to his towel.

"Uh…"

"Dammit," he said, realizing what she might be thinking. "Give me a few minutes, will you? I just have to…" He pointed toward the bathroom.

"Um, yes, um…" She looked around the room, trying to focus on anything but him. "I'm going to put the rest of my things in Jock's room, and then I'll go to the store. Duke's there waiting."

"Sounds good," he said. "I'll see you in, say, half an hour. I'm working the late shift so Sandy can take off early."

Without another word, Nora hustled to the door and away from the sight of Geno's torso. He had looked good in his twenties, but now he was all man, and she felt a primal pull toward him. She had to get out of there. Quick!

She nearly tripped as she ran down the stairs. Why hadn't Sandy warned her that Geno was here? More importantly, why hadn't she warned her that the man had a five-alarm torso? If he had been a fire, or wind, or some other force of nature, she would have had fair warning.

When the bell over the door tinkled again, Duke came running. He barked and wiggled as though she had been gone for weeks rather than minutes. She bent down to greet her little prince before straightening again and looking around at three new people in the room.

"Oh, hello," she said.

"Hi," said a young woman indifferently. "We thought you were Eugene."

A second said, "I'm here to sign up for guitar lessons."

"So am I," said the third.

"And me," said the first.

"Sorry to disappoint, but I'm sure he'll be along soon."

"We'll wait," said one, standing close to the front door.

"He said he'd be in a bit later today," said Sandy, eyeing the trio. "I can look at his schedule to see what he has available."

"No," they said, "we'll wait."

Sandy smiled like a Cheshire cat and raised her eyebrows at Nora. "Did you see Eugene when you were upstairs?"

Nora's mouth went dry at the thought of the man. Honestly, he had no right to look that good first thing in the morning. She nodded slowly. "Oh, yes," she said. "I saw Geno." Then, realizing they were all staring at her, she added, "I'm sure he'll be along in a few minutes. Meanwhile, why not look at the music books and see if there's something you'd like to learn to play? I'm sure there are several beginner's lesson books in here."

She bustled past them, forcing them to follow her. Once she'd shown them the best books to consider, she returned to Sandy.

"Thank you, dear," said Sandy. "Jock always said you were the mistress of the upsell."

"Glad to be of service," she said, giving a small bow.

Sandy chuckled, then said under her breath, "He's going to need it."

"Pardon?"

Sandy looked up from the schedule she had been staring at and cleared her throat. Was something upsetting her?

"Do you think Eugene will be long getting down here?" asked Sandy. "I'd forgotten how much of a draw he's always been to the younger women in town. He only got here two days ago, and they're already booking lessons with him."

"He was heading to the shower when I last saw him," Honoria said, not looking the woman in the eye. "I thought he would have found someone and settled down by now."

"No. He teaches snowboarding in winter, does construction in summer, and plays music in between. A Gene of all trades, he is."

Honoria noticed the young women were listening to their conversation.

"Well, I guess it is a benefit to Jock that he doesn't settle, and"—she lowered her voice so only Sandy could hear her— "it's probably a draw for all these women to see if they can be the one to tame him."

"Tame who?" a deep voice asked from behind them.

"Eek!" Nora jumped at the sound of Geno's voice behind her, and Duke yapped crossly until she picked him up to calm him. She was grateful for something to do. When she stood again, the little dog was still put out and wriggling to get away. "Where did you come from?"

"I came through the back room," said the grinning Eugene.

Nora looked between him and the curtain that led to the back room. She had forgotten about that door in her haste to get out of the upstairs apartment.

She was about to say something when the bevy of Gen Z-ers rushed toward them.

"I'm here to sign up for guitar lessons," said the one who reached Eugene first. The pushier one, noted Nora. The one who likely always got what she wanted in life. She wished she had learned to be pushier. Maybe then she would have children, a marriage that worked, and a faithful husband. Instead, she had none of the above.

"*We're* here to sign up for lessons," said a second, glaring at her friend. "We all want lessons."

"Oh," said Eugene, putting his arms on the counter and leaning toward them. "A group lesson sounds great."

The way he said it almost sounded obscene to Nora's ear. He was flirting with them, and they were lapping it up.

"Oh, no," said the first. "I want a private lesson. I think I would learn so much more that way, don't you?"

Nora turned to Sandy and rolled her eyes as she set Duke down on the floor again. The little dog went back to the corner where he had been curled up before Eugene had arrived, circled three times, and promptly closed his eyes again.

Sandy kept her face neutral, but her eyes were laughing in response. Meanwhile, Eugene continued to speak to the women about the music they wanted to learn, rang up their purchases, and let them know that a group lesson was the only way he could fit them all in. They must have liked the way he delivered bad news because each one turned around one more time before leaving the store. "Bye, Eugene," they said in chorus. "See you on Thursday."

"Bye," he said in return, and waved them off.

The door opened, and the bell tinkled, waking up Duke again. He barked a little at the noise and looked at the adults.

"Who does he belong to?" Eugene walked over to give him a pat.

"Duke is mine," said Nora. Actually, he was technically half hers, but Crispin hadn't asked for his visitation rights for weeks, so she had claimed him.

"Hi, Duke." Geno scratched his ears. "Nice to meet you. Good-looking dog, Nora." He stood again and nodded toward the door. "My schedule is nearly full," he said to Sandy. "I think we should leave off booking in more until we see how much work the festival is going to be. When did the mayor say the planning meeting will take place?"

"The next one was supposed to be this week, but she's canceled it. She'll reschedule once she's back."

"Back from where?"

"No idea," said Sandy. "But wherever it is, she's in cahoots with Virginia—and that woman is a menace."

Eugene raised his eyebrows in question as his gaze met Nora's. She shrugged in response. What Sandy had against those two women was a mystery to her, and she had no interest in walking into what promised to be a hornet's nest.

"I'm sure I can take on some lessons," she said instead. "I used to teach sax, piano, some voice, and the occasional kazoo or recorder." She laughed.

"That will come in handy for the children's show," said Eugene. "Do we have all the kids registered for that?"

"Yes," Sandy said. "I capped it at forty this year and raised the age minimum from four to seven. Last year was a disaster."

"Because Jock likes to start them as young as possible?" asked Honoria with a smile. Her uncle's philosophy was that if you got a child to love making music when they were a toddler, they would love it all their lives. Of course, Jock only taught preteens to adults, and he left his staff, chiefly Sandy, to look after the younger children.

Sandy smiled and rubbed her hands together. "But he's not here, and he left me in charge, so I'm doing it my way for once. Honestly. The man couldn't say no to a bout of swine flu."

"When do we really expect Jock back? What did the doctor say yesterday when you were there?" asked Eugene.

"It will probably be a week or two until he can leave the hospital."

"Does he have the insurance to cover it?" asked Nora.

"I don't think so. Well, I don't really know," said Sandy. "I've been trying to find all the papers, but his office is a nightmare."

"What did he say when you asked him?"

"None of your business, woman," said Sandy in a voice that sounded remarkably like Jock's. "Don't worry about it."

"Would his accountant know?"

"His accountant fired him after he showed up again last year with a box full of receipts and no organization. Old Max Baker had a lot of patience, in my opinion, to get through as many years as he did, but his son has taken over the accounting firm now, and Justin doesn't have time for that. He's going after bigger clients now."

"You mean Jock still just keeps paper receipts?" said Eugene. "That's ridiculous."

"I know. I was hoping you could help now that you're here, Nora. You're an accountant. Could you help me move him into the twenty-first century? I don't even know where to start, and his taxes are due in a week."

"Where does he keep the records?"

Sandy pointed to the curtain. "Back here."

"Can you keep an eye on the store and Duke for a few moments?" Sandy asked Eugene.

"Sure," said Eugene.

Sandy led the way behind the curtain and down a small hall to the back office. Honoria stood at the threshold and scanned the room. Every surface was full of paper or small items: everything from boxes of guitar picks to paperclips and assorted pens.

"I can see why you don't know where to start," said Honoria, wondering how on earth Jock had kept the store going this long. She walked over to the general ledger on his desk and leafed through it. Then she glanced at the surrounding boxes. Each small box was labeled by month. At least he had done that much.

"This might take a while, Sandy. I won't have a lot of time to help in the store over the next few days."

"That's fine. Gene is here, and it doesn't really get busy until next month anyway. That's when we'll start booking in the summer program."

"I'd best get started, then," said Honoria, sitting down in the chair and pulling the general ledger toward her. She had a feeling this was going to be a long week. A very long week.

CHAPTER 6

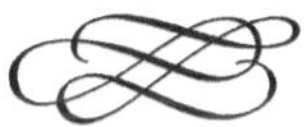

Sandy came back through the curtain, but Honoria didn't.

"Will she be able to help?" asked Eugene.

"I don't know," said Sandy. "But at she's got the skills to figure it out better than I can. I don't know why that man never listens to anyone."

"He's stubborn," said Eugene.

"If he weren't so wonderful otherwise, I would have left years ago." She started to cry, and Eugene pulled the woman close.

"Hey, what's wrong? I'm sure Nora will sort it out, and I'm here to help look after the store and teach the lessons. We'll do the best we can."

"I know that," Sandy said into his chest. "I'm just so relieved he's going to be okay and that you two are here to help. I wish you could stay longer, but the band will need you soon."

"Don't worry."

The band. He had forgotten about it in all the worry about Jock. The band would give him so much of what he craved: music, travel, and it would give his knees a rest. Because after twenty-five years on the slopes, his knees were demanding he take it easy. Roofing, with all the lifting and kneeling, only added strain to his injuries. If he could get a longer-term gig that only involved standing and strumming, well, no matter what his friends thought, he would welcome the change of pace.

"I hope Nora wants to stay too," said Sandy. "She could stay at my place if she didn't have a dog. They won't let me have them in the condo."

"Don't worry," said Eugene again, alarmed at the way Sandy was fretting. Sandy never fretted. He looked more closely at her face and saw dark circles and lines where she didn't have them five years earlier. "Listen, I'm sure Nora has had roommates before, and I'm pretty quiet. Besides, with both of us so close by, we can open the store in the morning. You can come in later. Get some rest. You've been doing double shifts since Jock's accident."

She looked up at him, her eyes searching his. "But what about your job? I don't want to be responsible for you losing your job."

"I can go later."

"But—"

"Enough," Eugene said, cutting her off before she could raise the objections he also had. How long would the band wait for him to sort this out? The pull was strong. It was offering him a big break after his years of noodling, and playing year-round for an established band would mean a lot less wear and tear on his body. "I don't have to be there for another few weeks, and I can practice in the lesson room in the back. Don't worry. I'll stick with you through this. You and Jock are my family, and after all you two have done for me, I'm just happy to help. I'm sure Nora feels the same."

As he said this, he realized it was true. Nora did seem to care for her uncle. Even all those years ago, whenever she visited Jock, she had been helpful with the children's concerts and beginner lessons.

"I hope you're right," said Sandy. "I'm worried it won't be enough to pay for his medical bills, much less a wage for the two of you."

"Let's not worry about things we have no control over. Nora will investigate the finances so we know where we stand. I'll run the store and take on Jock's lessons. You just need to focus on the festival and on getting some rest. Have you been eating okay?"

"Yes." She swiped her eyes with the back of her hand. "But maybe I should make some lunch. That might help."

"Great idea." Eugene squeezed her shoulder.

"I'll go upstairs and get us something. You can watch the store and the dog. I'll be back."

"Thanks," he said. "And, Sandy…"

"Yes?" she said, looking back at him.

"I know you're worried about him, but Jock's a tough guy."

"I know," she said. "But he's been burning the candle at both ends for months. I'm his only employee now."

"We're here now, Nora and me."

"Yes, but I don't know what he's going to do after that. I keep telling him he should sell the store and retire. But now?" She waved her hand toward the curtain. "I'm not even sure if the store is making any money."

"What about you? Are you able to retire?"

"Me? I'm fine. I own my house. I have savings. And I have my crafts."

"Crafts?"

"I make and sell pottery at an annual craft fair in Santa Barbara every year. It's enough to pay for my extras."

"Is there anything you can't do, Sandy?"

"Yes," she said. "I can't figure out how to help Jock make a go of this business. He took a chance on me when Blake died, you know. I hadn't worked in years, and this store gave me a whole new purpose in life. A reason to get up in the morning. I owe him so much."

"I'm sure if we put our heads together—you, me, Nora—we can come up with a plan."

"I hope so, Eugene. I hope so." Then she went through the back curtain to make lunch.

There was no one in the store, so Eugene followed her, stopping by the office where Nora was running her hands through her hair. He watched her for a moment as she jotted things down on a pad of paper. She looked so different from the Nora he remembered. The last time he'd seen her was the summer he turned twenty. He had fallen hard for a woman who was spending the summer in Cataluma. Elena had been gorgeous and full of fun: one of those women who collected admirers like his friend's grandmother collected charms for her bracelet. That summer he had mooned after Elena and had barely noticed little Nora, except as one would notice a pesky little sister who followed him around, constantly finding a reason to be in his presence. A gangly little girl who had not yet grown into her body.

Well, Nora was no longer a gangly little girl. She was a stunner. He watched her run her left hand through her long, dark hair. Her husband was a lucky man. Or was he? She wasn't wearing a ring. Why wasn't she wearing a ring? He cast his mind back to conversations about Nora and was sure no one had ever mentioned that she was going through a divorce. Maybe she was allergic to metal? Some people were.

"How's it going?" he asked.

She looked up, startled at the sound of his voice, and he noticed a thin gold chain around her neck. Nope. Not allergic to metal.

"I don't know, Geno."

He liked it that she called him that. It was warm, comforting. The only people to ever call him Geno were his mother and Nora.

"It's going to take me a while to figure out what's going on," she said. Then I'll have to see Jock in the hospital, see how he's doing, and go over it all with him. But on first pass, I'd say there's reason to worry."

"Let me know what I can do to help, okay?"

"Sure." She turned her attention back to the ledger and flipped over the page.

"Oh, and if you find the number for a tribute band in this mess, can you give it to me? Sandy said she'd looked, but she couldn't see it anywhere."

"I'll keep an eye out for it. Is it important?"

"Jock said he needed to confirm they were coming for the festival. That's all. You know him when it comes to shows and things. He pays a lot of attention to detail. I'm sure it's just a formality."

She looked up at him, doubt on her face. "I'll look for it. Maybe we'd better make sure." She cast her hand over the desk. "This mess does not give me confidence that he took care of that little detail."

"True." He watched her return to her work, and she looked up at him again.

"Sorry, is there anything else? Is Duke behaving?"

"Duke's fine. He's found a spot near the radiator and is enjoying a long snooze. I just stopped by to say that Sandy's making us some lunch."

"That's good," she said, her attention back on the books.

He stood and watched her a moment longer. When had she grown past her awkward phase, and why wasn't she wearing a ring? Her husband had to be crazy to let her go. He stepped back into the hallway just as she stopped and ran both hands through her hair.

"Uncle Jock, why didn't you say something? What am I going to tell Mom?" she asked the desk. He slipped away before she looked up.

He had to come up with a way to help Jock. Meanwhile, he would look at the lesson schedule. Maybe he could book another group or two. That could help.

When he walked back into the store, Duke pranced toward him, wiggling his back end in greeting. "Well, hello there," he said, bending over to pat the dog on the head.

"Hello?" said a voice from above.

"Oh, hello," he said, straightening up to speak to the young woman standing near the counter. "Can I help you?"

"My friend Sue said you give lessons," she said.

"Let's see what we can do," he said. It was only one person, but maybe if he got several more, he could help dig Jock out of debt.

CHAPTER 7

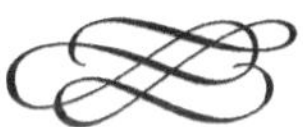

$\mathcal{N}$ora ran her hands through her hair for the umpteenth time that day and stared again at the numbers before she noticed someone else in the room.

"Well, hello, you," she said to Duke, who padded over to her and barked.

"Okay, thank you for telling me," she said. "Let's go get your leash, and we'll go for a walk."

She closed her laptop and rose. "Oh, ouch," she said, then stretched a few times before moving around the desk and glancing at the clock on the wall. It was six o'clock, and she had been here since ten, stopping only to go upstairs to Jock's apartment for her laptop and Duke's water dish, to eat a quick lunch, and to take Duke for a walk. Eight hours, and while she'd made some progress, it was slow going.

"Would you like something to eat?" she said to the dog. "You must be starved. I am."

Duke just wagged his tail and barked again.

"Yes, okay, I'm coming, I'm coming." She picked up the leash from the corner of the desk where she had left it, hooked it onto his collar, and walked to the front of the store to find it empty. Sandy and Geno had apparently left already. She walked to the front and assured herself that the door was locked, and the *Closed* sign prominently displayed, before going out the back way.

They walked several blocks before her stomach insisted she find something to eat. "Let's see if there's any food in the fridge at Jock's," she said to the dog, knowing she at least had dog food for the little guy. Maybe she could order a pizza tonight. It had been a while since she'd had pizza.

When she got back to the store, she climbed the stairs to the apartment, Duke bounding ahead of her, and was greeted by the scent of chicken, onions—and a hint of thyme or oregano, perhaps? By the time she arrived at the landing outside the apartment door, got to the top of the stairs, Duke bounding ahead, her stomach was growling audibly. What smelled so good?

"Hi," Eugene said when she came in the door. "You're just in time for dinner."

She looked around and took in the room. If she wasn't mistaken, it was much cleaner than when she'd left that morning. The dishes in the sink were now put away. There were no clothes on the floor, and there he was, putting glasses on the table— a table that was set with cutlery, plates, and even napkins. She could get used to this. Crispin had certainly never cooked for her. The most he could be counted on to do was to pick up takeout on the way home.

"I hope you like chicken cacciatore," he said.

"Love it," she said. "Let me wash up and give Duke his dinner first?"

"Of course. Take your time," he said. "I'll just stick the veggies on to steam."

Nora went to her room to get the dog food and a bowl to put it in. Duke pranced around as the kibble hit the bowl. "Ah, you are hungry," she said, laughing. She took the food out to the main room of the apartment—the room that served as kitchen, dining area, and living room—and set the dish in a corner out of the way. She stepped into the bathroom. The spotlessly clean bathroom. Wow! This guy was looking pretty perfect.

She washed her hands and returned to the dining area in time to see him place the chicken and veggies on the table.

"Do you want something to drink? I picked up a bottle of wine if you want one."

"That would be nice, thanks."

"Sit down. I'll get it. You've been working all day."

"Thank you." She sat down opposite him and waited for him to pour. "This is lovely. I can't remember the last time someone cooked for me."

"Your husband doesn't cook?"

She grimaced at the idea. "No. My soon-to-be ex-husband is good at a lot of things, including running his business, traveling, working out, negotiating deals—and cheating on his wife, of course."

It was his turn to grimace. "Sorry I asked."

"It's okay. We've been apart for almost nine months, and I suppose longer, considering he was with his girlfriend for three years, according to a mutual friend."

"Not much of a friend," he said. "They should have told you sooner."

"I don't blame Joanne. She was in an awkward position since she works for the company too and is a single parent. She didn't want to jeopardize that. He pays her well."

"Still. Three years?"

"In her defense, I don't know if she knew about it for that long. Anyway, it's done now. I just wish I'd known a lot earlier.

What about you? Do you have a significant other in your life?"

"No, I'm too much of a free spirit for that."

"Do you still teach skiing in the winter?"

"Snowboarding now, yes. And usually construction in the summer. It suits me."

"I couldn't do that. I enjoy staying in one place, putting down roots." She took a bite of the chicken. "Mmm, this is *so* good."

He smiled. "Thanks. I may cook for you again if this is the reaction I get. It's always nice when someone appreciates what I make."

"You can cook for me anytime," she said.

"Well, I enjoy it more than clearing up, so you may just have a deal," he laughed.

"I don't mind washing dishes," she said. "I notice the place is really clean. Did you do that?"

"Jock doesn't seem to make it a priority, so Sandy told me about a woman who could come in a couple of times a week. Today was her first day."

"Well, I say we keep her on. She did a great job."

"I agree," he said. "Now tell me…" His face turned serious. "What have you learned about Jock's situation? How bad is it?"

"It isn't great, from what I can tell. The business has been making enough to pay him and Sandy a wage, but there's not a lot of buffer. After so many years, I thought his situation would be healthier, but unless he has some other source of money I'm not aware of yet, I have to admit I'm worried about the hospital bills—and about how much he can realistically get for the place if he sells."

"Sells?"

"I know he's playing down the seriousness of his injury, but I'm not sure how long he can keep this up, especially if he needs a lot of physiotherapy."

"I can't imagine Jock without this store. It's always been part of the family."

"I know. Mom grew up in this store. It was their father's place."

"Right. I forgot your mom grew up here."

"Then she married Dad and moved north to start our own store. But even she isn't working full-time anymore. She's let my brother take over most of the responsibilities. Maybe Jock could take on a partner, too. I'm not sure how he would feel about that, though."

Eugene took a drink of wine and didn't answer. He just watched her eat, and the only sound in the room was the scraping of her fork on the plate. "Is that why you came instead of Robert? Because your mom needs help?"

"More because Rob's son is still in school for another couple of months, and because it's easier for me to work here. I've been living in the States for ten years. He's Canadian. Legally, it would have been more complicated."

"Ever think of going back?"

"Sometimes. Maybe after the divorce goes through. Meanwhile, helping Jock will give me something to do, and I'll be able to use my accounting know-how."

His brow wrinkled. "What about your job? Are you able to take the time off?"

"My last job was looking after the books for my husband's car dealerships," she said.

"Wow," he said. "So, when you broke up, you lost both your job and your relationship? What did you do?"

"I have a friend. She and her husband let me stay with her for a few months in their basement for a low rent, which was nice." She traced her finger around the rim of the glass. "But a basement suite in Seattle all winter sounds pretty depressing, so I'm glad to come down here."

"Did you not find work there?"

"I've always kept a few clients on the side, so that's helped. I filed the taxes for most of them before I left, and I can do any of the others over video call and internet."

"So you can do your job from anywhere?"

"Pretty much. Though I don't really like the laptop lifestyle. I miss being in an office with others. Being alone in the basement, waiting until my friend came home from work, and then only popping up into their space a few times a week so they could have family time…" She took a sip of water. "That was probably harder than having Crispin leave. My friend is happily married, has a couple of lovely children and a new baby, and I loved spending time with them. I even babysat a few times so they could have their date nights, but…"

"But it only emphasized what you are missing," he said.

"Yes, exactly."

"You never had children?"

"My husband didn't want any, and I thought, early in our marriage, that I could change his mind."

"I'm sorry. It's hard when couples have different priorities."

"Yes. But I wish he had told me before we married that he'd had a vasectomy. I thought it was just me. Wasted money on medical tests."

"You're joking. Why would he keep that a secret?" Eugene's face darkened in anger, and Nora smiled.

"Crispin is all about Crispin. I just wish I had figured it out years ago. I would have left him. As it is, he left me for his girl-friend, and I never saw it coming."

"No clues?"

"None," she said. "We were both working hard. After working long hours, I was so tired all the time. I tried to take on extra clients to help the business, and hire new people to help, but it was difficult. Then, eighteen months ago, he told me he was having an affair. We even went through couple's therapy, but in the end…" She shrugged.

"Breakups are always hard," he said.

"Especially when you are the dump-ee," she answered, yawning. It had worn her out to dredge all this up again, but Eugene was a good listener. She was grateful there was a table between them. It had been such a long time since a man listened to her—truly listened. If he touched her right now… Well. She didn't want to be responsible for her reaction.

"It's good, then, that you have Jock's business to focus on," he said, standing and picking up the plates.

"Hey," she said. "You cooked; I should do the clearing up."

"Let's make an exception tonight," he said. "You only arrived today, and we put you straight to work. You must be beat."

"Yes, I am." She handed him her empty glass. "I think I'll take Duke for a last walk and then go to sleep early."

He took the glass from her and turned toward the sink. She watched him surreptitiously for a moment, gawking like she had when she was fifteen. He hurried to put the leftovers into containers, rinse glasses, put the dishes in the dishwasher. The muscles in his arm rippled as he scrubbed, beckoning to her to come and touch them. Just as she was considering walking toward him, pressing herself against him, and seeing if he might be interested in more… she felt a cold nose on her shin. She shifted her gaze to find Duke smiling up at her. She chuckled. Caught ogling a man by the other male in her life.

"Okay, Duke," she said. "Let's go out." She went to the sideboard in front of the door where she had left his leash, and his little feet click-click-clicked over the wood laminate floor after her.

"See you later," said Eugene. "And thanks for coming, Nora. I know Jock appreciates it."

"See you," she said, then opened the door and followed Duke's lead down the stairs. She would have to watch herself around Eugene. He was a nice man. Gorgeous to look at. But he was a free spirit, and if she ever got involved with another man, she wanted one who would settle down and commit to her. Maybe even help her build a family. At forty-four, and with his lifestyle, she didn't see Geno being the one to do that, and she didn't have time for dalliances. She was forty, and if she wanted a family, it had to be soon. She might even have to do it alone.

She followed Duke as he pranced down the street, drawing smiles from passersby. No, no matter how lovely Geno was, she had to keep him at arm's length and remember her priorities. She needed roots. He needed wheels and snowboards. She was only attracted to him because he was kind when Crispin hadn't been. And maybe because he was a little dangerous with his motor-bike and tattoos. Unlike her rigid, clean-cut ex, who wore sharp suits and expensive cologne, Geno smelled like plain soap and water and wore relaxed jeans and a black T-shirt— casual clothes that fit him and reminded her of Vancouver Island, where she'd grown up.

That was the difference. Eugene reminded her of home, that was all.

And it had been too long since she'd felt like she was home.

CHAPTER 8

Eugene watched the door close behind Nora and her dog and felt the crackling tension leave with her. He plunged his hand to the bottom of the sink and pulled out the stopper, then quickly wiped up the counter. He had to get out of here before she came back. The woman was too gorgeous for her own good, and after hearing the woeful tale about how her ex had treated her, all he wanted to do was hold her in his arms all night long and touch her. Every single part of her.

Satisfied that the kitchen was clean enough, he grabbed his leather riding jacket, picked up his keys, and left. If he hurried, he could be several miles away by the time she returned—and he could find an excuse not to return until he was sure she was in bed. Asleep.

He turned his bike toward the bridge that led out of town and over to a strip mall. He would get some coffee and pick up some eggs and milk before coming back, and if that didn't take long enough, he could always walk over to the pub to watch a game or shoot pool. It didn't really matter. He just needed to get away from her sad eyes and that silky dark hair he had been itching to touch all evening.

Even her dog was too cute for words.

He pulled into the parking lot of the local Walmart and grabbed a cart as he walked through the doors. He walked up and down the aisles, picking up what he came for and adding other items of interest to his cart. Since he was cooking for two for the next few weeks, it might be fun to try some recipes he'd come across on the Food Channel this past winter. He'd noticed Jock's kitchen left a lot to be desired in the seasonings department. There was salt, pepper, and a little basil and oregano. That was it. No cumin, coriander. Not even rosemary.

He grabbed some spices and pushed his cart forward, nearly running into Sandy. He remembered only then that she had been over to see Jock after work. He blushed, ashamed that his focus had been away from Jock and firmly on Nora all day. He needed to keep his priorities straight from now on. And Nora was not his priority—Jock was.

"How did you find him?" he asked. He kicked himself again. He could have at least said hello.

"He should be ready to leave the hospital in a few days."

"A few days? That's earlier than we thought, isn't it? We'll need to find him a place to stay."

"He's agreed to stay with me," she said, her attention on the shelves. She was looking up at a box of baking soda on the top shelf. "Can you grab that for me?" she asked him, stepping back so he could reach for it.

He placed it in her cart.

"Are you sure you're up to having him there? I can ask Aaron if I can rent a place at the inn for a few weeks."

"It's okay. It'll be fine. This way, I can make sure he's eating and doing all the exercises he's supposed to do. Besides, Doris said she'd come down and help if I really needed it."

"You're in touch with Jock's sister?"

"Of course. Who do you think keeps the family up on what's happening with Jock? You know how he is about reaching out to others."

She had him there. Jock never had been very good about connecting unless Eugene phoned him. He'd never realized it was probably Sandy who reminded him, like a personal assistant. But she wasn't his personal assistant, and she wasn't family. She was an employee.

"It's not your job to look after all the details of Jock's life," he said. "If anything, it should be my job."

She placed her hand on his arm and looked up at him. "Really, it's okay. After all Jock has done for me over the years, it's the least I can do."

Eugene knew Jock had always received the larger benefit of that relationship, but he said nothing. With running the store, trying to turn a good profit, and getting ready for the Strawberry Festival, Eugene had enough on his plate. And Nora. She still had several days of work to do on Jock's finances. He patted Sandy's hand, grateful that she was able to help Jock in this way.

"As long as you promise me you won't let him run you ragged. And that you'll cut back your hours at the store. Maybe Nora and I can do it for a few weeks on our own."

"We can talk about the details later," she said. "I may want to come to work. Your father can be a bear when he's sick."

Eugene laughed. "Yes. Yes, he can."

"Thanks for helping me with the baking soda," she said. "I should go now. I have a lot of work to do to prepare for him to come home."

"Like what? If you need any construction-related work done, let me know."

"I will have to install grab bars in the shower and near the toilet," she said.

"Consider it done. I'll come over after the store closes tomorrow and take a look," he said, feeling relieved that he could do something useful to help Sandy.

"That would be wonderful, Eugene. Thank you."

Eugene finished shopping, loaded the groceries onto his bike, then drove over to grab a decaf coffee from Starbucks. He sat there until nine o'clock and decided it was safe to go back to the apartment.

Nora would surely be asleep by now.

CHAPTER 9

ora awoke to Duke whining and glanced up at the clock. Seven thirty!

"I'm sorry, boy," she said. "I slept in. Let me pull on some clothes, and we'll go out right now, okay?"

The little dog just whined again and pranced around the room as though he wanted to cross his legs.

Nora yanked on some jeans, stuffed her nightgown into the waist, and pulled a sweatshirt over her head before forcing her feet into her sneakers and grabbing the leash. "Come on," she said, pulling open the door and rushing over to the front door.

"Good morning," said Eugene, who was sitting at the table, sipping coffee and reading something on his e-reader. It must have been funny because he was barely holding in laughter.

"Morning," she mumbled, spinning away from him. "We'll be back soon. He has to go out before he has an accident."

"Okay," he said. "If I'm not here when you get back, there's porridge on the stove, coffee in the pot."

"Thanks," she said, and nearly lost her footing as Duke yanked her toward the door.

"Can we get together over lunch? I want to discuss the festival: get your ideas, figure out what needs to be done."

"Sure." Duke yanked at the lead again. "See you soon."

"Should have set the alarm," she mumbled to Duke as she walked the dog around the edges of the parking lot behind the store. "But it wouldn't have been a problem if that dream hadn't been so… vivid." She blushed as she remembered the dream that had awakened her in the middle of the night. The dream of Eugene, naked to the waist, entering her bedroom, reaching toward her, and promising a night of passion. Of love.

"Get yourself together," she grumbled as she cleaned up after Duke. "He doesn't even live in the same state. He travels. And he's no more interested in you than he was when you were fifteen. Besides, he's technically your cousin, for goodness' sake."

Duke barked at her, perhaps thinking she was talking to him, or perhaps telling her it was time to eat.

"Yes, okay, I'm coming," she said, stopping to toss Duke's package. Then she walked back to the house and climbed the stairs to get breakfast. When she got to the door, she saw her reflection in the glass. Her hair was everywhere. No wonder Eugene had given her such a strange look when she left. Great. Duke barked again, reminding her she still had to open the door. When she walked in, she found the apartment empty.

He'd probably left to avoid having to listen to her pour her heart out again. She'd sounded pitiful the night before, even to her own ears. Well, it didn't matter what he thought. She was here to help her uncle, and that's what she would do. She put food out for Duke, who ran to the bowl and began to munch right away. Then she hit the shower.

Forty-five minutes later, feeling fresh and fed, Nora settled into the back office to begin on the books again. Duke curled up in a ball beside the door to keep watch.

It felt like only a few minutes later when Eugene stuck his head in the room.

"Lunch?" he asked. "There's a restaurant nearby. My treat. We were going to discuss the festival. I want to get your ideas before I set things up."

Duke opened his eyes and looked up at him, then closed them again. Eugene seemed to have won him over with the little bits of chicken she'd seen him slip under the table the night before. Duke never bit the hand that fed him.

"Let me take him out first," she said, closing her laptop down and grabbing for

Duke's leash. "Can I meet you there?"

"Sure. I'll see you in a few minutes."

When Nora entered the restaurant after depositing Duke back in the office, it did not surprise her to find the server, a twenty-something woman, lingering at Eugene's table. The man was a magnet.

As she approached, the woman reluctantly backed away to give Nora room to sit. "Coffee?" she asked.

"Yes, please," said Nora.

"I'll be back in a minute," said the server, walking away.

"Another admirer?" Nora asked, focusing on the menu. She didn't want to examine why she was irritated.

"Another student," said Eugene. "She's joined the group tomorrow afternoon."

"It was a good idea to give group classes," said Nora, still looking at the menu. "We could use the business."

"It's that bad?"

"Yes," she said, closing the menu again and looking up at him. "I'm not sure what happened, but business seems to have been slow the past year, though he's still paying Sandy and he's still drawing a wage."

"Why didn't he say something?"

She shrugged. "No idea. Maybe he had a plan to turn things around."

"Like the festival?"

"It's one place where he gets his summer students," she said. "I found the numbers from last year, and they seem to be quite lucrative."

"Was he teaching them all himself?"

"No. He still hires college students who come back home for the summer, from what I can see."

"That makes sense." Eugene turned toward the server, who was returning with a coffeepot, and waited until she had poured them both a cup and taken their orders before he returned to the conversation.

"So how bad is it really?"

"I'm still sorting through the information, but it doesn't look good. He doesn't seem to replenish stock, and he's taking on fewer clients."

"Any idea why?"

"All I can think is that he's either not able to afford the new stock or he's winding down. Has he said anything about retirement?"

"Wouldn't it make more sense to sell a business that is a going concern? Or do you think he wants to sell the entire building and buy something else? Has he renewed the other leases?"

"Leases?" asked Nora.

"I'm pretty sure Jock owns the entire building and the stores on either side pay him rent. Though I could be wrong. I have to admit, I never really paid much attention to it when I was younger. It was always his business."

"I'll look. I thought he just owned the store and the apartment above, but maybe he's got some other income he tracks elsewhere. I'll finish sorting through everything I have this afternoon and start on the tax forms. Once I've gone as far as I can, I'll go to the hospital and ask him. I haven't actually been up to see him yet. I only talked to him on the phone. And my mother is itching for an update once I've seen him in the flesh."

"And you'd best get Doris what she needs as soon as possible," laughed Eugene.

"So you remember my mother?"

"Hard woman to forget," said Eugene. "She is a force to be reckoned with. Much like her brother."

Nora laughed. "They do have that in common. They take after their father in that regard."

Eugene chuckled, remembering his grandfather. "Meanwhile, Jock's asked for help with the festival, so I don't think he's planning on winding down just yet. I've made a list. Can we go over it, see if I forgot anything?"

"Sure." She took the list from him and scanned it, then spent a pleasant hour sharing a meal with Eugene and brainstorming ideas. When they were done, they walked together to the store.

"I'll run this past Sandy this afternoon," he said. "See what she thinks."

"Sounds good. I'll be in the back if you need me for anything." Then she walked through to the office, patted Duke on the head, and hoped Eugene might have a reason to come looking for her.

CHAPTER 10

"I'm going to see Jock," Sandy said as she turned around the *Open* sign and locked the front door. "Can you close out today?"

"Sure," said Eugene. "I'll get a start on inventory as well. I notice we're getting low on some of the grade one guitar books. Is Jock still using the same system?"

Sandy rolled her eyes. "Yes. He keeps track of it all in that green book behind the counter. I've told him there are easier ways to do it these days, but he refuses. He thinks his new till is bad enough."

"Maybe Nora can help us convince him."

"Maybe Nora can help you convince who of what?" Eugene turned to see the object of his thoughts come through the hallway curtain with her little dog prancing ahead of her. She looked a little tired, but she was smiling.

"Jock's stock-tracking system needs to be computerized," said Sandy. "And since you seem to have a knack for the digital end of things, we thought maybe you could help us talk him around."

"He would say he keeps it all up here." Nora laughed, tapping the side of her head. "And I'm sure after all these years he probably has a good sense of things, but I agree with you. It sure would make year-end accounting easier if we could just track it on the computer."

"How are the books coming along?" Sandy asked, looking wary.

"I've almost got the taxes done. There are a couple of regular outgoing payments that I'm not sure of, so I don't know if I can deduct them or not, but otherwise, I'm close to the end. If I'm right, the bill will be relatively small this year—but that also means the profit was smaller."

"But he's still turning a profit?" asked Eugene.

"He is, but not enough to make much more than a living wage. And I have found no record of leases and such. I still wonder if he isn't trying to wind down the business."

"What?" asked Sandy. "What do you mean?"

"I don't think that's what he is doing, but the stock is pretty low, and he doesn't seem to purchase more."

"You said there are payments you don't understand?"

"Yes."

"I'm going to see him. If you give me the list, I can ask."

"Actually, I was planning to go too."

"But I have some personal things to discuss with him," said Sandy.

Why was Sandy speaking in staccato? Eugene stopped watching the conversation as though it were a game of tennis and said, "Why don't we all go? I have a couple of things to ask him too. Then Nora and I can go grab something to eat."

"I think we should take two cars," said Sandy. "That way, if I need to leave, I won't have to wait for you. I have a few other errands to run."

"That sounds great," said Eugene. "Is that okay with you?" He turned to Nora, who simply nodded, as though all the words had been sucked out of her.

"I'll have to take Duke, though. I can't leave him alone in the house for too long, especially if I don't know how long it will take. He's good about sleeping in the back seat. I just need to grab his water dish and some kibble. He'll be good to go."

"I'll see you there, then," said Sandy, turning to leave the store through the back way.

"Did I say something wrong?" asked Nora, watching her leave.

"I don't think so, but she didn't sound like herself."

"So you noticed she seemed short with me, especially when I suggested coming with her?"

He nodded.

"And what kind of personal things does she have to discuss with Uncle Jock?"

Eugene considered her question for a moment. "Maybe the idea—that her job may be gone if he winds down the business—put her shirt in a knot."

"But she doesn't really need to work, does she?" Nora asked as she walked toward the back door.

"I always thought her husband left her pretty well off, but maybe I'm wrong." Eugene followed her a few steps then remembered he had promised to close up. "Listen, I have to cash out the till. Why don't you take the dog for a walk and get his things, and I'll get the bank deposit ready. We can drop it in the night deposit on our way out of town."

"Sure," she said. "I'll meet you out at the car in about thirty minutes."

When Nora had gone, he thought over the conversation he had just witnessed. Nora was right. Sandy was acting strangely. In fact, she had been acting strangely for a few days. Maybe it was just worry about the store. He and Nora were going to have to plan how to pick up the slack.

It would give them something to talk about as they drove into town. He went around to the till, cashed out, recorded the day's receipts, and rushed out the door. He was looking forward to spending time with Nora again, but he needed to keep things cool. He was sure Jock would object to any relationships between them. Jock was lackadaisical about most things, but Eugene had a feeling he would be a real stickler when it came to his niece. Especially since his niece was going through a divorce and was vulnerable.

But when he thought of the way Nora carried on conversations with her dog, and the way she scrunched her nose when she went through her uncle's books, he knew he was smitten.

Why did he always have to pick the wrong woman?

CHAPTER 11

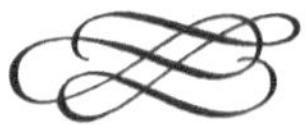

Nora rolled down the windows and waited for Eugene. Duke lay in the back seat, happily gnawing on a treat she had given him, so she had a few moments to herself.

She used them to text herself a question that had come up about Jock's taxes—and to keep her mind off the elephant in the store that would be sauntering toward her any minute. Why did Geno have to look so good?

Today he was wearing a tight black T-shirt that only reminded her of the torso she'd seen two days earlier. It also revealed his tattoo that read, *Where Words Fail, Music Speaks.* That was one of her favorite quotes about music.

He would be here any minute. She had to stop with these musings. The man was family, for heaven's sake. What would her mother say? What would Jock say? She shivered a little as she imagined Jock bellowing at the two of them—just like he had bellowed at her and Robert when they were younger and got into mischief. Jock no longer towered over her—and he was, at present, an invalid—but she didn't want to hurt him.

No, she would have to keep the elephant outside of her life. He could visit as a friend, but that was all. Besides, hadn't he said he was leaving soon? And she would also have to go, eventually. Start her life again. Find another job. Maybe even go home to Canada. There was no reason to stay in the States now that her husband had left. She would have to investigate what she would need to practice in Canada. Tax laws were different, but she had done most of her education in Vancouver. She was typing out a reminder to call the tax association when she heard a knock on the passenger window. With a yelp, she looked up to see Eugene's hazel eyes looking back at her.

Duke yapped again, and she shushed him, ignoring the prickles that traveled down her spine as she quickly reached for the buttons to unlock the passenger door.

"Got everything?" she asked.

"Yep." He held up the deposit bag, opened the door, and slipped gracefully into the seat beside her. She stared at his thighs for a moment, then remembered she had promised herself to keep him at a distance. She quickly started the car and shifted into drive.

"Do you know how to get there?" she asked. "I had to use GPS last time."

"I can direct you," he said. "We won't get lost. I can even drive if you like."

"Maybe on the way back," she said, pulling onto the street and stopping at the first traffic light.

"Works for me." He shifted the seat back so there was more leg room. She watched him out of the corner of her eye until she heard a loud honk behind her, reminding her that the light had turned green. Duke barked back at the honking horn, and Eugene just chuckled.

Face warm with embarrassment, she put her foot to the gas and followed the road to the bank.

This was going to be a long trip.

CHAPTER 12

$\mathcal{A}$fter stopping at the bank, Eugene sank back into the passenger seat and relaxed. It had been a long time since he'd been in the passenger seat, with the luxury of not having to watch the road. He took some time to look out at the scenery —and away from Nora.

She was wearing a dress, and her sweater kept slipping off her shoulders. He wanted to reach over and pull the sweater back where it belonged, covering those gorgeous shoulders. Better to look at the strawberry fields and vineyards as they rolled past.

"How is your brother doing?" he finally asked.

"He's a lot better than he was when April died. Being a single parent is hard, especially when he was so sure she'd beat her cancer."

"And how old is his son now?"

"Zack is ten. I haven't seen them in over a year, but I do video calls with them once or twice a month, and Zack plays his sax for me. Sometimes I play with him. It's kind of like being there. Kids his age are fun. I'm looking forward to working with the festival kids again this year."

"I enjoy them too," he said.

"Did you ever want kids yourself?" she asked, then mentally kicked herself. She hated it when people asked her that question. It was so insensitive, and it always felt like people were judging her for not having children.

She was silent for a few minutes, focusing on changing lanes and passing the car in front of her. Finally, after sliding back into the right-hand lane, she said, "Sorry, I shouldn't have asked that."

"No, it's okay. I wanted kids once. When I was younger, I was head over heels in love with a woman I was sure was the one. Unfortunately, she decided my friend was the one for her. They're happy, and they have four kids."

"That must be hard."

"Yes, but I've enjoyed my nomadic life, and kids would have been harder to fit into my lifestyle."

"What's that like?" she asked, and he spent the rest of the trip telling her stories of the places he'd been on his bikc, the people he'd met, and life on the ski hill. It sounded like he'd had a fun life, but underneath all the stories of adventures and friends, she couldn't help but notice a certain twang of loneliness. He was alone in the world except for Jock. And the thought of him all alone made her ache for him.

"Take the next exit," he said half an hour later. "The hospital is just off that road."

They pulled up to the hospital, and she found a nearby spot to park and got Duke out of the back seat. "I'll be right back," she said. "Just taking the dog for a little walk."

Eugene watched her walk across the parking lot to a small patch of grass. Then he unfolded his legs and climbed out of the Mini to stretch. The car was a little cramped but still comfortable enough. He looked in the back seat and noticed the dog's dish was nearly empty, so he opened the back door, opened a bottle of water from the floor, and poured some in just in time for Duke to come bounding back, his whole backside wiggling. "Well, hi there," Eugene said, laughing at the little dog.

"He likes you," said Nora, picking up the dog and putting him in the back seat. "Thanks for filling his water bowl."

"Not a problem."

"It was a problem for Crispin," she said, rolling down the back window enough to let in air, though the sun was nearly set.

"Some people are just not good at remembering things," he said. He had learned never to throw a woman's ex under the bus. In his experience, it always backfired, whether he agreed with them or not. Best to stay neutral. But it felt nice that she'd noticed and appreciated his little helping gesture.

"Perhaps that was it. Perhaps he just forgot things," she said. He could tell by her tone that she didn't believe it for a moment.

"What are you doing, going through my papers?" Jock roared at Nora when she walked into the hospital room. He and Sandy were both red-faced, as though they'd been in a heated discussion.

Nora arranged her face to neutral and answered as best she could, thanking the stars for her early career experience dealing with internal audits.

"I'm taking over as your accountant because I was told the last one couldn't take on the work this year."

"He would have come round."

"Well, judging by the phone call I made to him a couple of days ago to get some background information, I would say that would have taken longer than we have."

"His father was easier to deal with. Never been the same since that young whippersnapper took over the company." Jock glared at her.

She glared back. "Well, lucky for you, I'm here, and I have a lot more experience with this sort of thing than a young whippersnapper."

"She is doing a very thorough job, Jock," said Eugene.

"Yes, well…" Jock sputtered.

"I'm setting it up so it will be easier for the whippersnapper next year. I'll show you and Sandy some of the work I've done when you are feeling better and are ready to come back to the store." Sandy looked stricken, and Nora continued, "Really, Sandy, it's easy. I'm sure you'll get the hang of it in no time, and Jock will hardly even have to speak to the whippersnapper."

Sandy looked at Jock, and Jock looked back at Sandy. Sandy nodded at him.

"We will not learn how to do that," said Jock. "I'm selling the store."

"What?" said Eugene. "Why?" He came over to sit in the chair on the opposite side of the bed from Sandy.

"Doctor told me it would take me at least another six months to feel like myself. The hip and my arm…" He held up his cast. "It may take longer than they first thought."

"So you're going to sell the store?"

"Yes," said Sandy. "And when he gets out of here, he's going to come and stay in my extra room. Jock has done so much for me since Blake died that it's the least I can offer."

"And Sandy can't run a store, get me back and forth to appointments, and all the other things she does."

"So you're looking for a buyer, then," said Nora. "All the more reason to have the books done and updated onto a computer system."

Sandy turned toward him and squeezed his hand. "It's for the best, Jock. It will help a new owner to know what's what, and to give them some idea of what they're getting themselves into."

"What else are you changing behind my back?" Jock grumbled.

"Well, I've started giving quite a few more group classes," said Eugene. "That will make the takings look great going into summer, when the students can come back and take on lessons again."

"That's good, yes," said Jock. "And the festival?"

Nora looked over at Sandy, who jumped in first, probably worried Nora would spill the beans about raising the age limit. "Nora and I have our first lessons with the children on Monday after school. I've auditioned most of them, and I am happy to say we have quite a few coming back this year."

"Are you two able to handle it all?" he asked.

"I'm not going anywhere," said Eugene. "Not until after the festival and the current block of group lessons is done."

"What about your job?" asked Jock.

"And the band?" Sandy looked concerned.

"What band?" asked Nora.

"There's a circuit band in LA. I was going to join and travel around California with them over the next few months. If I can make it work, I won't have to go back to snowboarding. Boarding's done a real number on my knees the past couple of years."

"Well, if you hadn't taken up jumping…" Jock growled from his bed.

"Perhaps you're right." Eugene smiled at Jock. "But I am pigheaded, you know."

"Wonder where you learned that?" said Sandy under her breath. She looked at Eugene and Nora. "Well, I'm going to grab a coffee. Nora, why don't you talk to your uncle about what you came here to talk about? Gene, you come with me."

Eugene rose, and Nora watched them both walk out of the room before turning toward Jock.

"I just have a few questions," she said, opening the messenger bag she had brought with her. "There are some payments I don't understand." She took the seat Sandy had just vacated.

"I wish I could get him to take over the store," said Jock, looking wistfully after the departing Eugene. "I always kept it here for him. Thought maybe…"

"But can you afford to even retire if you don't sell? Especially with your medical costs?" asked Nora.

"Nora, I'd like you to do my other taxes for me as well. To do that, you'll need access to the safe in my room upstairs."

"What safe?"

"The one behind the big picture of the moose near my bed."

"I like that picture," said Nora.

"It always reminds me of Canada," said Jock. "I'm considering going there to retire, you know."

"People from Canada retire here, Jock, not the other way around."

"Well, never say I'm not an original," chuckled Jock. "It would be nice to be near your mom and Robert. I miss having family around. Don't tell me you never think about it."

"I do," she said, shifting in the chair and rustling through the papers to find the notes she wanted to ask about. "But I don't want to be chased away just because of one rotten marriage."

"That's my girl," said Jock, patting her hand with his good arm. "You always had a lot of gumption."

"I haven't heard that word in forever," she said, grinning at him. "Thanks for saying that."

"Do you think you could make Eugene see that Making Sweet Music would be good for him? It would be nice to leave it to someone in the family."

"I can try," said Nora. "But you know Geno. He's a free spirit. Hard to pin down."

"He doesn't need to be pinned down," said Jock. "He just needs a reason to stay." His eyes drifted to the doorway again, and Nora could tell his thoughts had taken him down the hall to his son.

She patted his arm, and he turned again toward her. "Let's get this technical stuff out of the way so I can finish up these taxes tomorrow. Then I'll do your personal ones as well."

"Right," he said. "There's a key to the safe in my room at the top of the kitchen cupboard in the mouth of the owl there."

"High-tech security, eh?" Nora laughed.

"Would you look in an old China owl for the key to a man's fortune?"

"No, can't say that I would," said Nora. "Fair point."

"And please don't tell Geno about it. Not yet. He doesn't know what my situation is."

"What exactly is your situation, Jock?"

"I'll let you be the judge of that," said Jock. "Once you calculate what's there and do my taxes for the year, come back."

"Okay… No hints?"

"You'll understand when you see it all. My insurance papers are in there too. I'll need you to bring them. The accounting office is hassling me, and I need to show them my supplemental coverage. It's a wonder anyone gets well having the stress of money to worry about in these places."

"Why are you trusting me with this?"

"Because, as my accountant, you have to keep things confidential."

"So I'm your accountant now, am I?" she teased.

"Make out a check for what it costs to do all this while you're at it. That way, it will be official, and it will give you some walking-around money until you get paid through the store."

"I can't take your money."

"Yes. You can." He growled at her. "Promise me."

She nodded just as they heard footsteps coming toward them down the corridor: loud footsteps made by biker boots and softer footsteps made by sneakers. "And, Nora, don't tell Sandy. She doesn't know either."

"Sure," she mumbled softly, collecting the papers together as the pair walked back into the room. In a louder voice, she said, "Thanks, Jock. I think I have everything I need. I'll be back tomorrow or Thursday with the papers for you to sign." She rose, bent over the bed, and kissed his unshaven face.

"Thanks, Nora," he whispered. "I'm counting on you."

She smiled tightly then stepped away from the bed, allowing Sandy to take her seat again.

"Eugene, I'll meet you outside. I'll just go check on Duke."

She walked past him, and Eugene sat down beside Jock again.

As she walked down the hallway, she wondered what Jock had in the safe in his room and what his insurance covered. It made her want to go directly home. But instead she would have dinner with Eugene. She had to try to convince him to stay in Cataluma—to make him fall in love with life there.

She would start by getting him more involved in the community. Maybe look for a suitable woman? Her gut roiled, and she quickly put the papers in the trunk and got Duke out of the car. She was hungry, and she hoped Eugene would hurry.

Eugene sat across from Nora on the restaurant patio, where they allowed dogs, and considered how to talk to her about taking over the store. Sandy had told him it was Jock's suggestion. Jock thought it should stay in the family. Robert couldn't do it. He was running his mother's place. But Nora—now that she was single and at loose ends, maybe she could do it. She had worked in retail most of her life, and she understood the financial side of things.

But would she want to? Eugene sat in silence, looking out at the street and trying to think of a way to bring it up.

"It was a bit of a shock to think of Jock selling up," said Nora after they'd ordered. "I can't imagine Making Sweet Music without him."

He turned toward her, startled at how easily the subject had arisen. "Yes, it would be great if someone in the family would take it over, but I'm not sure who. Robert can't do it. You said yourself he's got a life there."

"It would be a good thing if someone could take it on," said Nora.

"Yes, a rewarding business. Fun, even," said Eugene.

"Yes, it would," she said enthusiastically.

Maybe this would be easier than he thought. "Though running a business takes a lot of unique skills. There would always be something to learn."

"There would," agreed Nora. "But that would be the fun of it—and there would be the opportunity to teach children. They are so much fun to work with, and music is excellent for their development."

"Exactly. The business would be an opportunity to hone the skills and creativity of the next generation," said Eugene, taking a drink from his water glass.

"I should write all this down," said Nora, "to help sell the business." She pulled out her phone and typed, writing the pros of owning the business. "We should also write the cons so we can counter them if people come up with objections. How about 'the town is too small'?"

"We could flip that: it's inviting, cozy, community minded. Welcoming, even. A town where everyone can be anything they want to be."

"I like that," she said. "And it's true, isn't it? Cataluma is a nice place to live."

He smiled. Yes, this conversation was going very well indeed. "Okay, here's one. It's hard to find clientele for music stores, especially in such a small town."

"Oh, that's an easy one. There's no competition in Cataluma, and both the schools rent their band instruments from us. We've had a great partnership with them for years. And Jock has always found good-caliber talent to teach lessons. We have a strong music program in this town."

"In fact, didn't he teach Luke James? The country star?" he said.

"Yes, and little Emma… what's her name…" She snapped her fingers, trying to remember.

"Emma Lockhart," said Eugene. She's been singing in Broadway plays for the past five years. You're right—she got her start with Dad, too. Someone taking over the business would need to find new teachers. Or be able to teach themselves."

"True. But there are a couple of people in town who are qualified. I found a list of people Jock uses when he gets classes going in September," said Nora.

"So, if you can get the books up to date…" he said.

"And the stock system under control." She frowned.

"We could do this. Get it ready for the next owner."

"Right," she said.

Did he sense disappointment in her voice? Did she, too, hate the idea of selling to someone else? Maybe Sandy was right. Maybe Nora would be a great owner for the store. She had it in her blood, after all. She'd grown up in one. If he kept her involved, maybe she would come around more easily than he thought.

The meal came then, and she put the phone away.

"I know we're trying to get this ready for sale," she said. "But I wish there was a way we could keep it in the family."

"Would you consider buying him out? Consider settling down here?" He watched as she considered her question.

"No, I don't think so."

"Maybe I could at least get a good friend interested," said Eugene. "I know a couple of guys that might like to settle down here. Put down roots."

"You think one of your friends might buy the store?"

"I can ask." He looked at her to gauge her reaction. Is that what she wanted? Or did she hate the idea of someone other than family taking over? It was hard to tell.

"Meanwhile, our food is getting cold, so why don't we eat?" she said. "We have a lot of work to do before we can put it on the market anyway."

"Exactly," he said, slipping a piece of bacon from his burger to the dog.

"No wonder he likes you so much. You're his new treat source." She laughed at how Duke looked up at him adoringly.

"You never know when you might need a friend," said Eugene, slipping the dog another little bite. "It's not like you get unconditional love very often."

"True," said Nora, her face becoming pensive. "That's what I like about Duke. He's never let me down. Not like…"

"Hey," he said, placing a hand on her arm. "Don't dwell on the past. Not all men are like that. You'll find a new relationship when you're ready."

"I suppose," she said. "Meanwhile, it is nice to have a project to focus on. That was the most frustrating thing about finding out about Crispin. I had given up my career to work for the dealership, and then I lost that too."

"Well, I know Jock appreciates what you're doing. He was singing your praises after you left."

"That's sweet of him," said Nora. "I really hope we can make the store attractive to a potential buyer. It will help him retire and move on to what he wants to do next, wherever that is."

"You think he'd move?"

"He might. He was talking about going to Canada."

Eugene sat back in his chair as though pushed by some unseen force. "He'd move?"

"Well, without the store, he doesn't have much to keep him here, does he? You travel all the time. He would be alone."

"What about Sandy?"

"What about her?"

"I always thought there was something between them."

"Maybe," said Nora, patting Duke, who was whining at her feet. "There's food in the car for you," she said. "You've had enough bacon."

Duke looked up at her, then gave a little huff before turning around three times and lying down his back toward her.

Eugene laughed. "Looks like he would prefer bacon."

"You've created a monster," she laughed. "When you leave, he'll go into bacon withdrawal."

He laughed at that, but his gut felt empty. *When he left*, she'd said.

But did he even want to leave?

Eugene drove them home after their meal and Nora drifted off to sleep, listening to the radio. He looked over at her and smiled at her little snore, which sounded remark-ably like Duke's coming from the back seat. It was nice to have them here, in this place, together. When he finally pulled into the parking lot behind the store, he was hesitant to wake her. She looked peaceful. The furrow in her brow had smoothed, and for the first time since she'd come, he was seeing her with her guard down. She was even smiling in her sleep. *What I wouldn't give to know what she's dreaming about.*

Huh. Why was he so interested in knowing more about Nora? She was his cousin by marriage. He needed to avoid this relationship like he'd avoid a nasty virus, but he couldn't but help wonder what it would be like to kiss her right now. What it would be like to have her wrap her arms around his neck.

Duke stirred in the back seat and barked, saving him from his treacherous thoughts, but Nora still caught him looking at her when she opened her eyes.

"What?" she asked.

"We're home." He turned his attention to removing the key from the ignition.

"Oh." She straightened up in her seat and twisted to undo her seat belt. "I'm sorry I fell asleep. It's a habit when I'm a car passenger."

"It's okay. I had the radio to keep me company, and I'm used to driving solo." He waved his hand toward the Ducati.

"I suppose that's true," she said. "I hadn't considered that." She was looking at him with those eyes he'd noticed the first day. Those eyes that used to be in the body of a fifteen-year-old girl who was way too young for him.

She wasn't too young now.

His gaze drifted from her eyes to her lips, and he swallowed hard, forcing his gaze back to her eyes. Nope. She was not that gangly girl anymore.

"Um," she said, not moving, though there was no reason to continue sitting in the car.

"I guess…" he said, but the rest of his sentence didn't make it out of his mouth because her lips were pressed against his and her arms were curling up behind his neck. He pulled her close, and she sank against him, filling a need he had been denying for too long. They kissed for a long time, out there in a dark parking lot only steps from heated rooms and comfortable beds. He thought of adjourning there but thought better of it. The woman was going through a divorce. She was vulnerable.

She was his cousin! The thought crashed into his brain like he had hit the water during a polar bear swim. He stopped, pulled away. "We shouldn't do this. What would Jock think?"

She sat back, looking a little stunned at the sudden change in position. It took a moment for her to answer—a long moment when he just wanted to go back to what they'd been doing.

Finally, she said, "Right. You're right. It could get messy." Though she didn't look like she believed her words. It looked like she, too, wanted to pick up where they'd left off.

"And you are coming out of a divorce."

"Yes. But you aren't the rebound guy, if that's what you think. There was a…" She shook her head when he grinned at her. "Never mind. It was nothing. It only lasted a few weeks."

"Glad I'm not that guy, but I think we should remember who we are and what we need to do."

"Yes, you're right. But I was feeling comfortable around a man for the first time in years, enjoying your company."

"I wish it weren't complicated too. I just think we should pretend this never happened."

"Okay. Let's do that," she said, looking at him one last time with longing before turning to open the door and climb out of the car. "Can you pop open the trunk? I have to get Jock's papers before I forget."

"Sure." He leaned forward to press the button then sat back a moment, closing his eyes and trying to wipe the memory of her swollen lips from his brain. Forgetting that kiss was going to be impossible. The best he could hope to do was focus on helping Jock, talking Nora into staying in Cataluma, and then exiting stage left as soon as he could.

He undid his seat belt and climbed out of the car, thinking that the next few weeks—until the Strawberry Festival was over, until Jock was home, until he could finally escape—would be long weeks indeed.

"Come on, then," she said to Duke as she coaxed him out of the car.

He had never envied a dog before, but as she accepted the dog kisses and laughed with joy, he scowled and walked toward the apartment, leaving her to follow behind.

CHAPTER 15

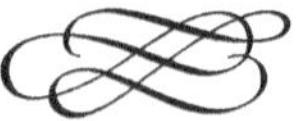

$\mathcal{N}$ora walked Duke around the parking lot while mentally scolding herself. What had gotten into her? A dream about Geno looking down at her as she slept, waking her, and pulling her into his arms. It was a dream come true that had turned into a nightmare. How would she ever face him again?

Jock would be livid if he knew, and he would probably blame Eugene because, as much as Jock loved his stepson, he often bemoaned the fact that he wouldn't settle down. Jock, who had been in a band in his youth, who had filled Eugene's head—and hers—full of tales of the open road, was now reaping what he'd sown and was asking her to fix the damage.

How would she ever convince Eugene to stay in Cataluma and take over the business? Why would he want to? And now she wouldn't even be able to speak to him without remembering the feeling of his arms around her. She had never felt like this with Crispin. Holding Geno had felt comfortable. Welcoming. Like it was all going to be okay. Like she belonged.

Or maybe it was that Geno accepted her for who she was and didn't try to change her. Crispin had forever been critical of the way she dressed, the way she wore her hair, even her ideas. Crispin had made her feel small. Geno, by contrast, made her feel okay just being herself. With him, she felt capable and strong. It had been a while since a man had accepted her for just who she was.

And it had been a while since she had accepted herself for who she was. Eugene and Jock, and even Sandy, were good for her. They believed she could help turn the business around. Help figure out Jock's taxes. Jock had trusted her even with information about his safe and his secrets. Whatever they were.

They were her family, and they were there for her.

That was all it was. Eugene was family, and he treated her just like a loving family member did, and she was confusing things by kissing him. Glad she had given herself a stern talking-to, she took Duke inside and locked the door behind her. The apartment was quiet, and Eugene's bedroom door was closed. Good. It would give her time to retrieve the key to the safe without having to answer questions.

After putting water out for Duke and filling his dish with kibble, she pulled the old owl down from the top shelf and reached inside for the key. She found only a piece of paper with numbers on it. She pocketed it, then carefully placed the piece of crockery back where she'd found it. Duke's nails clicked on the hardwood floor as he followed her around the house while she got ready for bed. Once she was in the bedroom, he curled up in front of her door and promptly fell asleep, snuffling softly.

Nora stepped around the dog, carefully took the moose picture from the wall, and set it aside to get a better look at the wall safe. She punched in the numbers from the paper she'd found and opened the door. The safe was a small compartment that held nothing but papers. Whatever Jock had said was valuable was not immediately clear.

Grabbing up the pile from the safe, she sat on the bed, spreading the papers out in front of her, trying to put some order to what was, in true Jock fashion, a creative filing system. She found the health insurance first, looked it over and made a note of questions she had to ask him about rehabilitation coverage. Then she moved on to a group of papers that outlined Jock's investment portfolio, a sealed envelope with a copy of his will, old mortgage papers showing he owned the building outright, and a bank statement from the previous month that showed regular deposits into an account to cover rents from tenants. So he owned the building, just as Eugene thought. And though the rents were pretty low by the standards of a larger city, they were enough to give him a good income.

Jock wasn't hurting for money. Not one bit.

She looked at the other papers and identified investments, tax forms, and all the information she needed to file his taxes. After making another list of questions to ask Jock, she picked up a large brown envelope labeled *sheet music*.

She pulled out the papers inside, each one in its own protective cover. Her eyebrows rose as she leafed through them. Jock had music from jazz musicians. Sheet music that looked old, maybe even the original or early editions.

She wondered how long he'd been collecting. Her brother Rob would love these. Besides classical, jazz was his favorite type of music. She closed her eyes and thought of her brother, and his dream of being first chair in the symphony had been dashed.

Life never quite worked out the way you planned, but he still had his son and had given their parents a grandchild. She didn't even have that. All she had was the task of helping Jock get Eugene to take over the store. She would put her all into this job and then decide what to do when summer ended. When she had to go back to her real life. If only she knew what and where that was.

Gathering the papers together, she put them back into the envelope. She had laid one worry to rest. She didn't have to worry about Jock's financial future anymore. He could retire anywhere, especially if he went to Canada where his dollar would go further. But she didn't want to get ahead of herself. Maybe if Eugene took over the store, Jock would decide to stay on. That would be nice for Geno. To have a place to call home. To put down roots.

She put aside the bank statements and investment information and put everything else back into the safe, replacing the picture on top. She would figure out his personal taxes in the morning after finalizing the business taxes, then drive back to the hospital to talk to Jock.

As she drifted off to sleep, she wondered how Eugene was doing, and how she would ever get him to take over Making Sweet Music. All she could do was get him involved. All she could do was try.

CHAPTER 16

Two days later, Eugene was saying goodbye to his last group of students when Sandy stopped by the classroom. "Have you thought about what I said?" she asked.

"Yes," said Eugene. "But why not just ask her if she'd like to take it on?"

"Because she needs to be invested, and the only way to do that is to get her involved in our community. When are we going to meet to discuss tactics?"

"I have some time now. Want to grab a coffee?" Eugene put his guitar back into its case and stowed it behind the door so he could practice later. He needed to get more time in with his instrument if he was going to catch up with the band in a month's time. They had found a temporary replacement, but they wouldn't wait much longer than that, and he had to be familiar with their music before he joined them.

"Sure," she said. "Why don't we go out the back? I've already locked up, and Nora is doing some work in the office. I don't want to disturb her."

"Or have her know you are plotting against her?" He fell into step behind Sandy and followed her to the back door.

She turned to him once they were outside. "I prefer to think I'm plotting *for* her. It's in her own best interest to find a place to settle down—away from that stuffed shirt she was married to. That man broke her heart, and I know Jock is worried about her too. He's asked her to take on a friend's taxes this week, and if she sticks around, she may get a lot of smaller referrals from the whippersnapper." She started walking toward the Copper Moon Restaurant.

"Hold on," said Eugene. "I'm confused. Are you telling me that Jock would be okay with her starting another business? And closing Making Sweet Music?"

"Well, ideally, it would be the music store. That's what Jock would prefer. Music is in the family blood, after all. But he just wants to get her back on her feet. He's always had a soft spot for Nora. Ever since she and Robert used to spend time here in summer."

"But she can set up a tax business anywhere. Even back in Seattle."

"Yes, but…"

"But what?"

They reached the coffee shop. She waved two fingers at Paul, who was working behind the counter, and sat down. "Well, here's where I'm being selfish, I suppose." Her face reddened.

"You? What are you talking about?"

"I don't want Jock to leave, Eugene. If he can't even get into his apartment because of the stairs, and he can't run the store anymore, what's left for him here?" She looked around the room, then leaned forward to whisper. "He's talking about going back to Canada. To Sunshine Bay where his sister lives."

Eugene sat back and stared at Sandy for a moment. What would Cataluma be like if there were no Making Sweet Music—no Jock?

His home base would be gone.

While he would probably see Jock just as often, Vancouver Island would not be home. He looked Sandy in the eye. "Then let's figure out a way to stop that from happening. We'll sit here and drink enough caffeine to send us to the moon if we must. He accepted the cups of coffee the harried server brought over to them. "Let's plan."

Sandy looked visibly relieved and twisted around to pull a pad of paper, a pen, and a calendar out of her bag. She uncapped the pen and flipped the calendar to the day and date. "Okay, let's get started." Eugene smiled to himself. With Sandy on his side, they would make this happen.

He could practice tomorrow.

CHAPTER 17

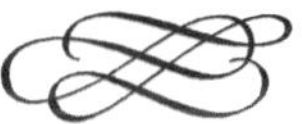

"**Y**ou're not ready?" Eugene said when Nora emerged from her room the next morning wearing a bathrobe and slippers and rubbing her eyes.

"Ready for what?" They didn't have plans she was aware of. She snapped the dog's leash onto his collar and went toward the door.

"We have a big day of festival planning," said Eugene, walking over to take the lead from her. "Let me walk Duke. You get ready. We're going to a planning meeting, then we're going to meet the rest of the vendors to talk up what we're trying to sell this summer. And we need to plan for our summer staff—make sure they're all returning."

"Uh…" She reluctantly handed the leash to him and nodded. "Sure. I'll shower and get dressed." As she watched Geno and Duke head down the stairs, she smiled to herself. Maybe getting Eugene interested in staying on would work out after all.

A half hour later, they left Duke in the apartment despite his whining.

"He does that to make me feel guilty," said Nora. "As soon as I'm out, he'll find a place to curl up and forget all about me."

"Let's go see Sequoia at the bakery first," said Eugene. "I'm hungry, and he makes a great scone. Then I'll take you down the street and introduce you to everyone. It helps to know all the businesspeople on the street. Maybe we'll find some opportunities to collaborate, spin off some business from the festival, or hear some news that will help us make the business more of a going concern."

"Do you know these people?"

"Most of them. People stay in Cataluma once they get here. It's a great place to live. Raise kids. That kind of thing. Many have been here for years. And some took over the family business. I know them from school."

"I know barely anyone I went to high school with. I miss that: knowing people who have known me my whole life. There's a certain comfort in old friends."

"There's also a lot to be said for new friends. Usually, we have more in common with them because we're meeting them as they are now instead of as ten-year-olds."

"Still," she said, "I sometimes wonder what it would be like to go home to Vancouver Island. I miss the ocean when I'm not too close to it."

"Is that why you chose to live in Seattle?"

"No, I picked Seattle because that's where Crispin's from, and he worked in the family dealership. I wish I'd known sooner that we weren't meant to be. Perhaps my life would have ended up differently, and I would have a career, family, and children half-grown by now. Maybe I'd be a soccer or hockey mom, running the store with my brother."

"Would you like to run a music store?"

"In a different life, maybe. You?'

He stopped talking for a moment. Then, just when she was sure he hadn't heard her, he said, "You know, perhaps I would have enjoyed it. If Jock had asked me to come back and help him, I wouldn't have said no. I never wanted him to have to look after me, and I didn't want to encroach on his territory. But if it were my own place, like a franchise or something? Yes. I might have enjoyed that."

"Might have? What about now? Why not think about taking over the business?"

"I can't really afford to buy him out. I have some savings, but if I need to help him with his medical costs…" He shrugged.

"Maybe you could pay for it over time. Give him an income for a few years. We haven't really talked about how much he would want for the place. Maybe he would be okay with installments."

"Installments for fifty years?" He laughed.

"I don't think it would take that long. Why don't we talk to him? Find out what he wants for the place. Then you could think about running this one. He's going to sell anyway."

"It would be better with a partner," he said. "Someone to help. I would need to find staff. It's a lot to think about."

"But surely you've supervised others—taught them how to teach snowboarding, for example."

"Yes, I've done that for a few years, but…"

"But?"

"I don't know. I would need to give up my band if I were going to do this."

"Or you could find another way to do that, too—to do what you enjoy most about the band."

"What do you mean?"

"Is it the music, the performance, the travel? What is it about the band that draws you to it?"

After a few moments, he said, "I've never really thought about it."

She glanced at him as they walked. "Have you ever thought of settling down here?"

"Me?" Another question he didn't know the answer to. Did he want to come back to Cataluma? Would he settle down?

"Yes, you. Do you ever tire of moving around? You aren't a tumbleweed. You're human."

He opened the door to the bakery. "Here we are. Why don't you get that table by the window, and I'll get something to drink? Coffee?"

She nodded, peering over his shoulder at the table and then twisting to look at the counter. "I'll take a scone too, if you're offering." She pointed at a platter in the display case. "I like the ones with blueberries best." She sat down at the window, took out her phone, and scrolled through her messages and emails.

~

"What can I get you?" Eugene turned to find Sequoia grinning at him. "Food-wise, I mean. I can't help you over there." He nodded toward Nora, and Eugene felt his face heat.

"She's Jock's niece," he said. "My… my… cousin." He had a hard time getting the word out as he remembered the kiss they were not talking about. The kiss that had ruined him for other kisses. The kiss that had felt so right and had recurred in his dreams the night before, making him awaken in a sweat.

"Isn't she more like a step-cousin?" Sequoia said. "I think if you wanted it to go further, people would be fine with it."

"Not Jock. He's really protective of family. Particularly Nora."

"I guess it depends on where it's going."

"What do you mean?"

"Well, if it's a quickie, then not cool. If it's a relationship, you want one that lasts. You may have something there. I mean, she's already settling in here. I know two small businesses that are ready to jump ship now that Justin's taken over his father's accounting business. She treats everyone like they matter. And she knows her stuff. Really."

"She's been here less than a week."

"I know, but Sandy has been singing her praises, and then Brett got her to do the books for his sports store. And I overheard a few people in here talking about her. I think she'll have a growing business if she wants it."

"But that's not music."

"No, it's not. But music is more your thing anyway, isn't it? Yours and Jock's. Maybe you should come and settle down. Help him out. It may take him a while to get back on his feet."

"Is Sandy your source of information for that, too?"

"No. I may have heard that from Mildred or her friend Virginia. Not sure. Anyway, it stands to reason that if he's taken a fall that landed him in hospital this long, the physio will take a while."

"That's why we're here. Helping him out. I'll stay as long as it takes to get him back on his feet."

"Well, that's good. Meanwhile, the town is happy to have a new small-business accountant in Nora. Now what do you want? I'm getting a line."

Eugene looked over his shoulder to see a few people waiting, so he quickly ordered and walked back to join Nora, who was in conversation with a woman he didn't recognize.

"Hello," he said, waiting patiently for the woman to rise from what was supposed to be his seat.

"Oh, hi." The woman with spiky auburn hair looked up at him. "I'm sorry, is this your seat?" She rose.

"This is Patricia from the library," Nora said. "We were just talking about me coming in to give a brief presentation about taxes at one of their lunch programs." She turned to Patricia. "This is Eugene. He's Jock's son."

"Oh, so you're the famous Eugene." Patricia chuckled. "I understand you have quite a few new students."

"We like to think music is for everyone," Eugene said, shaking Patricia's hand.

"I just hope it takes with some of your students. Maybe you could get a band program started or something. Too many of them are at loose ends during the summer. It would be constructive."

"We'll have to think about it. Right now, Nora and I are getting ready for the festival. But thanks for the suggestion." He sat in her vacated chair, and Patricia turned to thank Nora again. "Listen, I'll come by in a day or so to see what you decide. I hope you'll do it. There are so many people who need help now that Max Baker has retired. His son…" She rolled her eyes. "Definitely not a chip off the old block. Has a lot to learn if he's going to keep his business going here."

"We've heard." Eugene laughed. "And if Nora needs some time off from the store to help, we'll make it work."

"Oh, thank you," Patricia said. "Thank you both." She rushed out the door just as their coffee and scones arrived.

As they were drinking their coffee and munching on baked goods, Eugene chuckled again. "Here I was thinking you'd need introductions, but it looks like half the town knows you already."

"I have a feeling a little bird has been singing my praises. I just hope I don't disappoint her."

"Sandy is hard to disappoint."

"It feels like she wants me to stay on. The longer I'm here, the more it feels like she wants me to stay permanently."

"What about you? What do you want?"

"I don't know." She took a sip of coffee and looked out the window at some children skateboarding past. "I like it here. When Mom asked me to come, I was happy to help Uncle Jock and get my mind off Crispin and the divorce. But it's just what I needed. I didn't realize how much stress I was under while I was in Seattle. Since I left, I feel lighter. More relaxed. I hadn't even realized how much energy it took not to think about him. But everywhere I went reminded me of what I lost. Being here, I've barely thought of him. I even played my sax for a few minutes last night. I haven't taken it out of the case in over three years."

"Making music again. That's great," said Eugene. "And you could do worse than Cataluma. Setting up business here could be good for you. Jock might even let you set up in the store."

"You mean close Making Sweet Music? No. That would be horrible. I can work anywhere. Out of my house if I have to. But the town needs a music store.”

“Would you consider running it?”

“Me?” she squeaked. “I know how to teach little kids, and I know something about music, but I’ve been in the car business for the past fifteen years. The learning curve. I mean, it would be huge.”

“But you could do it.”

“Maybe if I had a partner or some really reliable help.”

“If you did it, it would stay in the family.”

“Well, if you took it on, it would stay in the family, too.”

“Don’t look at me like that,” he said. “Making Sweet Music isn’t in my life plan.”

“And you actually have a life plan?” she asked, a skeptical look in her eye.

"Right now, my plan is getting a job in a band. Traveling."

"You're always moving around. Why haven't you settled down in one place?"

"I have tried a few times, but the women I meet usually want to settle with a man who is more established. I made the mistake of introducing them to friends, including one who owns a tech company and, well, what would you choose?" He moved one hand up in the air. "Ski bum who is virtually homeless or"—he held up the other hand—"multimillionaire who can give you a mansion and a stable life?"

"Well, I've had the rich husband. It's not all it's cracked up to be," she said. "I'd rather have the one who loves me and wants to spend time with me. The one who wants to be my family."

"Oh," he said. "Your ex is rich?"

"He owns four dealerships, and his father comes from money. It's all about the bottom line in Crispin's world. My accounting side appreciated that. It looked, as you suggest, stable. But stable can also be a constraint if it comes with the need to always be perfect. If you can't be who you really want to be."

"What couldn't you do?"

"I'm not cut out to be a corporate wife. I wanted a small business of my own, the opportunity to really make my own way. Getting it all handed to me was stifling."

"So you would be interested in starting your own business?"

"I have a small business already. Always have. But I could never grow it to anything more than a side hustle. Crispin got me running the accounting department for the company, and it became all-consuming. I learned a lot. It's just that when it was all over, well, leaving has been such a relief. I was that guy from Greek mythology, Sisyphus—the one who had to roll a boulder up a hill for eternity. Until the boulder suddenly vanished."

"And now? What's different?"

"I feel a lot less stress. I sleep better even though I should be worried about money. Though my lawyer says I should be okay. Crispin owes me half of what we got out of the marriage and, as the accountant, I know exactly how much that is. I kept excellent records."

"Is it going to court?"

"I don't think so. Right now, Crispin is just trying to keep the condo. I heard through my friend Joanne—the one I told you about—that he wants to renovate it. I got him to halt on that until he settles with me. Hopefully it will only take him a few more weeks."

"Sounds like he's there for the long term. Why doesn't he just sell and move? Can't he buy a condo anywhere?"

"Well, it's the penthouse in a swanky building downtown, so no. He wants that one. And I don't really care about it. I never felt comfortable there, anyway. All I want is for him to buy me out."

"But in the meantime, what are you living on?"

"I have some savings. My little business. A few new clients from Jock and Sandy. And free rent while I'm here watching over the store. So I'm okay."

"But I don't understand what's taking so long with the divorce. How long have you been separated?"

"I moved out nine months ago. Couldn't stand him bringing his girlfriend home any longer. We were in two different parts of the suite. It was painful to watch, and the walls were…" She held up her fingers and squeezed them togethcr.

"What a jerk."

"Anyway, I finally packed up my things, and Duke, and rented my friend's extra suite. He's never asked me about Duke, so I intend to keep him."

"Meanwhile, you just wait?"

"My lawyer is on it. Crispin is stubborn, but my lawyer is ruthless. The longer it takes, the more she calculates the interest payments." She looked at her phone. "It has been a few days since I heard from her. I'll have to follow up in the morning."

"Are you still thinking about going home to Canada after the settlement?"

"I don't really want to."

"No?" He felt relief at that.

"I would just become my mother's latest project. She'll try to fix me up with someone. And much as I would like to run interference for my brother to help him out, I'm just not ready to face that."

"Run interference?"

"Rob is Mom's project right now, from what I gather. Mom is trying to fix him up with anyone and everyone."

"Poor Rob."

"He's a big boy. Besides, Mom has now booked a cruise with my dad, and they're coming down to visit here on the way. She wants to check in on Jock—and on me, of course."

"When?"

"Dad's traveling for work, but when he gets back, they'll come. Next week."

"Will they be here long?"

"No. And while they are, I plan to get them to help us. Keep them busy. Then they can't work on *me*."

He laughed.

"Speaking of which, do you want to make that list now? I like to be prepared when it comes to Mom and Dad."

"I'm sure they can't be that bad."

She rolled her eyes. "When was the last time you spoke to my mother? She was bad enough when she was working full-time, but now that Rob has taken over the store, she's bored. A bored Doris is a dangerous Doris."

"Let's get that Doris-Do list started, then."

They spent the rest of the morning planning the music for the show and putting together the schedule. They figured out what stock to order for their festival table, along with what to print for schedules and what to charge—all while they continued their tour of the street. When they got to the inn, they ordered take-out burgers to eat in the park before heading home.

As they were leaving the restaurant, Aaron caught up with them. "Hey, Gene, I was just going to phone you. I need to confirm those three rooms for the festival band this year. Jock never confirmed, and with his accident, I forgot."

"Definitely," said Eugene. "We'll have a band."

As they left the inn, he turned to Nora. "Did you ever find the name of that band?"

"No, but there are some papers I haven't gone through yet. Maybe I'll find it this afternoon."

"I'll help. I'm sure Jock arranged things, but I need to be sure. The festival is only a few weeks away."

"Why don't we take the burgers back to the office and eat there? The sooner you find it, the sooner you can confirm."

When they returned to the store, it was just past noon.

"Where have you been?" Sandy asked as soon as they came through the door.

"I took her out to meet the townsfolk, and we've been planning," said Eugene.

"You told me you'd be here by eleven. Now I'll never…"

"Never what?" said Nora.

"Never mind," said Sandy. "I need to go. I have things to do." She ran out of the store and down the street.

"What was that about?" asked Nora.

"No idea, but I feel bad. She told me to be back by eleven."

A customer came into the store then, and Eugene turned to talk to them. Nora went to the apartment to take Duke for a walk, and the burgers grew cold.

At five o'clock, after Nora had finished the taxes and Eugene had closed the store, they finally had time to search the desk. "I can't find it," said Nora.

"I don't think it's here. He must have put it somewhere else."

"We'll just have to ask him."

"And admit that we messed up?"

"Do you see any other option?"

"No."

"He needs to sign his tax forms anyway. Let's go tonight. I'll grab Duke."

When they arrived at the hospital an hour and a half later, they heard raised voices as they approached Jock's room.

"Who's that?" asked Nora.

"Sounds like Jock and a woman."

They quickened their steps until they got to the threshold of Jock's room. Then Eugene quickly stepped back, pushing Nora behind him and forcing her to stand on tiptoes and peek over his shoulder.

"Who's that with Sandy?" she whispered. "What's going on?"

"That's Virginia. Shh," he said as they both strained their ears to understand what was being said.

"I don't care why you say you're here," Sandy hissed at Virginia. "I know the truth."

"What are you on about?" said Jock. "I don't know why you're so upset that Virginia is here."

"She's been here for over an hour, Jock! I saw her come in."

"So I'm not allowed to have company in the hospital?"

"Not her company." Sandy glared at the pair of them.

"Sandy, you need to stop," said Virginia. "This isn't what you think."

"Oh, really?" said Sandy. "So now you know what I'm thinking?"

Virginia put up her hands in front of her, trying to calm Sandy down, but Sandy wasn't in the mood to be calmed.

"I think she's finally snapped," whispered Nora to Eugene.

He nodded. "I wish I knew why Virginia was here. Are she and Jock seeing each other?"

Nora shrugged and turned back toward the room when Sandy raised her voice even higher.

"I don't care what you do, Jock. Sell the store, move to Canada, move in with Virginia! I'm done."

"Sandy!" said Virginia. "You've got this all wrong."

"No. You've been sneaking around together for months. I've seen Jock slipping into the back door of City Hall, and I've seen you slipping in the back door of the store. People don't sneak around if they don't have something to hide."

"Okay, you're right," said Virginia. "I have been hiding something."

"See! I knew it." Sandy spun toward Jock. "I've had it, Jock! After all these years of being there for you no matter what, I'm done. Consider this my official notice. You can figure out another place to stay when you get out." With that, she turned toward the door and stomped out.

"Sandy!" Jock yelled. "Come back! It's not what you think."

But she kept going toward the exit, not even noticing Nora and Eugene through the tears that were slipping down her face.

"What the heck?" said Nora. "What's going on?"

"I don't know," said Eugene. "I've never heard her yell before."

"Should we go in?"

"Maybe just hang back here a bit until they're done."

"Should we go get a coffee or something? Or stay here and listen?" asked Nora.

"What do you think?" he said, moving closer to the door so they could hear the conversation.

"I don't know what she's going on about Virginia, or why she's so damned upset," said Jock.

"Well, it's obvious to everyone else. I'm just sorry she saw us."

"What's obvious?" Jock asked. "I've never seen her so angry."

"You really don't know, do you?" Virginia said, shaking her head.

"No. Are you gonna tell me or just leave me in the dark?"

"Jock." Mildred sat down in the chair next to the hospital bed. "I hate to be the one to tell you this, but that woman, who has been your friend and constant companion for over twenty years, is in love with you."

"In love with me?" Jock looked at her as though she'd just turned into a rabbit.

"The question is, how do you feel about her?" Virginia said, patting his arm and then pulling an envelope out of her purse. "I should get going. Here's the money I owe you." She handed him the envelope, and he took it, his mouth still hanging open.

"Uh, thanks," he said, taking the envelope and putting it on the tray beside his bed.

"And thanks, Jock. I really appreciate you keeping this all under your hat, and I am truly sorry that it has caused you so much trouble. I'll be finished my little project in a few weeks, and if I'm successful—or even if I'm not—I want you to tell her. You two are good together, and I would hate to ruin that. I already hurt Sandy once before."

"What do you mean?"

"There was a boy in high school. Benny. He took her to the prom, but he took me home. I've always regretted how much I hurt her. We used to be friends. She's barely spoken to me in years."

"I had no idea," he said. "That's why she's angry with you so often?"

She nodded. "But don't worry about me. Just see if you can smooth things over with her. Really, you two belong together." She smiled at him sadly and then walked toward the door. Geno and Nora ducked into the next room.

"Did you bring my dinner?" a frail voice said from behind them.

They spun around to see a woman sitting in the bed, tiny amongst the pillows and blankets. "I'm sorry, someone else handles food," said Nora in a calm voice.

"Can you tell them I want an extra chocolate pudding tonight? I love the chocolate pudding."

"I can do that, yes," said Nora.

"Come on," said Eugene. "The coast is clear."

"Goodbye," Nora said to the woman, giving her a little wave before Eugene yanked her out the door.

She shook free of his grip and started to walk in the opposite direction. "Where are you going?" he said.

"To the kitchen to ask for extra pudding."

"What about Jock?"

"I'll catch up with you. He might prefer one person pouncing on him right now instead of two. Ask him about the band. I'll be back."

"Fine," said Eugene, and he walked the few quick steps to his uncle's room.

When he walked in, he found Jock lying down again—and appearing much more tired than he had only a few minutes before.

"Hey, Dad," said Eugene. "How are you doing tonight?"

Jock turned his face toward Eugene's voice and smiled wanly. "Pretty crappy, Gene." He turned away again, staring out the window.

"What's up?" Eugene searched his brain for something to say that wouldn't give away what he'd just witnessed. "Is the physio not going well?"

"What?" Jock turned back again. "No. It's fine. I'm going to be released earlier than they figured I would."

"That's good. It'll be nice to have you at home. I'll be able to see you more often."

"I'm going to need another place to stay," said Jock. "Sandy won't be able to help me like I thought."

"Oh, that's too bad. I'll see if I can get a room at the inn for a few days until I set up something more permanent. Do you think Sandy just needs a break? I can cut her hours back at the store if that would help."

"No. She's leaving the store, too. She quit."

"Just like that? Out of the blue?"

"Yes."

"I'm sorry, Jock. Is there something I can do? Did Nora and I make things too hard for her?"

"No. It's me she's leaving." Jock's voice cracked. "Just when I finally see what's been right in front of me."

Eugene walked over to sit in the chair by the bed. "Tell me what I can do to help."

"Gene, you being here will help. You and Nora. I don't know what I'd do without you right now."

"Well, you won't have to find out. And I'm sure Sandy will come around. Maybe she's just been under a lot of stress."

"No. She yelled at me, Gene. She's never yelled at me. Not in all the years I've known her. I've hurt her. I wanted to run after her, tell her how I feel, make her stay, but this damned hip." He swept his hand over his torso. "I can barely walk, let alone run."

"You're getting stronger every day, Dad. This is only temporary, and Sandy will come around."

"You didn't see her, Gene. She walked away, and she's not coming back."

"Why don't we focus on getting better? Getting stronger. I'll get a place for you to stay and look around for a rental. We'll get you back on your feet, then you can tackle Sandy. She's not likely to go far. She's been in town forever. You've got time."

Jock didn't answer for a long time, and Eugene thought perhaps he had fallen asleep. But then he said, "You're right. I can only focus on what I can control. I'll focus on getting out of this damned hospital, getting home, and getting better. Then I'll talk to Sandy. When I'm back to normal. When I have something to offer her again."

"Jock." Eugene patted his arm. "It will be okay. You and Sandy have been friends forever."

"That's just it, Gene. She doesn't want to be friends. She wants more, and I didn't even know it."

"And you? What do you want?"

"Gene, until she walked out today, I didn't know how much she meant to me. I need to get her back in my life. I love her."

Gene sat back in his chair. "Wow. That's quite the epiphany."

"Would have knocked me to the floor if I hadn't been laid up already. Why didn't I see it?"

"Because we get comfortable. Complacent. Used to the way things are."

"And we don't even see what's right in front of us."

"Exactly," said Eugene.

"Enough about me. How's the store doing?" asked Jock.

"It's good, but I need to ask you about that tribute band. I can't find the contact information, and I need to confirm it."

"You mean you haven't done that yet? You've been here a week."

"I know. I've been busy. And your filing system isn't exactly easy to figure out."

Jock scowled. "You sound like Sandy."

"Truth hurts."

Jock scowled again, then nodded in agreement. "The band. It's an Eagles tribute band we used before, a couple years back."

"Not To the Limit?"

"Yeah, that's the one. You know it?"

"It's the band I'm joining up with."

"They're good. That's why we're getting them back," said Jock. "Maybe they can be our regulars, and then I'll be guaranteed to see you at least once a year, eh?"

Gene laughed, but he didn't find the joke funny. Jock was only reminding him how little he had been around for his father. And he really had no excuse. He would do better. Be around more. Seeing Jock stuck in the hospital made him aware of how little time they might have left together. He had to make the most of it.

"I think I can do better than once a year, especially since the band plays mostly in California."

"It would be nice to have you around more."

"Are you really thinking of selling up? Moving to Canada?"

Jock shook his head. "I was hoping Nora would take on the business, but according to Sandy"—he swallowed hard—"Nora's been getting customers who need an accountant."

"She's taking all the whippersnapper's business, it seems."

"I'll have to come up with another idea for the music store. If I can get back on my feet soon, I can probably do it for a few more years. Maybe by then something will come up. And if Nora sticks around, I can share the back office space with her. She told me she's been running her business with just a laptop, so she won't need much room."

"That's true. And then you'd have family here," said Eugene.

"If she'd be willing to do it. Sandy was trying to convince her, but…"

"I know, Jock. But I'm still here for a few more weeks. I'll help."

"Help with what?" asked Nora as she walked into the room. Her face looked a little tight, and Eugene wondered if she had been hiding in the hallway, listening. And if she had, what did she think about the plans Sandy and Jock had for her?

"With the festival, and with getting Jock back on his feet," he said. "Jock says that Sandy has quit the store, so she won't be around to help. When he gets back to town, he'll be able to do some of the work, but his days will be shorter for a while."

"Sandy quit? Was it something we did?" Nora was pretty good at pretending she hadn't heard that conversation. It was as though they were both on the same page without having to say a word. It felt good to have a partner in crime.

"No, it was something I did," said Jock. "Here." He handed Nora the envelope Virginia had left behind. "Can you deposit this for me? It's for lessons."

"You give lessons in the hospital now?"

"It was a one-off. I've been working with someone for a few months, helping them bring up their skills so they can try out for a part. Don't ask me any more about it. I'm sworn to secrecy."

Nora took the envelope and put it into her purse. "Sure, I'll deposit it."

"Thanks, Nora."

"And while I'm here, can I get you to sign the tax forms? Unless you're too tired?"

Jock nodded. "I am tired, but I also don't want to pay a penalty for a late filing."

Eugene rose to give Nora the chair. "I'll be back in a few minutes," he said. "Going to grab a coffee. Want one, Nora?"

"Tea, please. And if they have a herbal one, could I have that? If I don't reduce my caffeine intake, I won't sleep."

"Tea it is."

CHAPTER 18

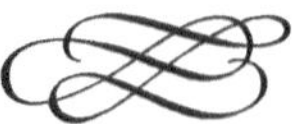

"Thanks for doing this, Nora," Jock said after signing the forms and the check she'd made out for her services.

"Not a problem," said Nora. "And when you get back to the store, I'll show you what I've put on the computer. It really will make things easier."

He grimaced. "Sandy has been encouraging me to move online for years. I should have listened to her. Should have noticed more."

"Sandy will come round. She's been working for you for years. She loves the music store. The kids, the festival."

"Yes, but she's been after me to consider selling for the past couple of years. Hinting that she's thinking of retiring. Talking about things she'd like to do."

"And do any of her plans sound good to you?"

"What do you mean?" He looked up at her.

"Uncle Jock, it's obvious that Sandy has feelings for you. Why else would she have stuck around this long? I mean, you are kind of grumpy. She must like you a lot to put up with that all the time."

"So I've been told. Why didn't I see it sooner?"

"Same reason I didn't see that my husband was cheating on me, I guess. Because we are busy in our own little world. Going through life one day at a time."

"Do you think you could help me get her back, Nora? She likes you."

"I can try."

"Thanks."

"Oh, and Uncle Jock? What's with the sheets of music in your safe?"

"It's a collection I inherited from Gene's mother. It's time I turned it over to him, though. I doubt he even knows about it."

"Is there anything you want me to do?"

"Find out how much it's worth. If he doesn't want to keep it, maybe we can sell it at auction. Right now, all it's doing is gathering dust. It's time I let go of it. It's time I let her rest."

"Okay. I'll look into it and let you know."

They were silent again, both thinking their own thoughts, until Eugene returned with the drinks.

"Time to go," he said. "We've got a long drive ahead of us."

"Yes, and a store to run." She rose and kissed Jock on his cheek. "We'll see you in a couple of days. Let us know when they're going to spring you from here."

"I will," said Jock. "It'll be good to come home."

"What are we going to do?" asked Nora when they were on the way home. "Can we even run the place without Sandy?"

"We're going to have to."

"At least the taxes are done, and I've got his books set up on the computer now."

"And your other clients?"

"There are only three, and from what I've seen of the first two, their records are pretty good. It shouldn't take me too long. I can even do them at night if I have to. It wouldn't be the first time."

"The store is pretty quiet in the mornings. Why don't you do them before noon and then we can work on the music side?"

"And your practicing? When do you plan to do that?"

"At night. After we close the store. You're welcome to join me if you like. Practice your sax?"

"I'd like that. I may come and jam with you after I get this work done."

"It would help me to keep time with another musician. I'm sure we can find some sax music for a few of the songs."

"Well, it sounds like we have a plan for the interim. Now all we need to do is figure out what to do with Jock when he gets home—and how to get him and Sandy to-gether again," said Nora.

"Maybe it can go on your Doris-Do list," laughed Eugene.

"Hey, that's not a bad idea." She grabbed his arm then quickly released it, but not before he felt the warmth, the connection, the attraction. "Mom knows Sandy," she said, turning to look out the window. "I'd even say they're friends. I'm sure she'll help."

"Doris to the rescue."

"It will give her another couple to focus on. Maybe keep her away from my personal life." But Nora didn't sound convinced.

"As long as we can get her to help with Jock. Now that he's coming home early, he'll need extra support. Your parents will be a big help, I bet," said Eugene, trying to sound encouraging.

"Yes, I'm so glad they'll be around for a few days. Maybe by the time they leave, we'll have the students back. College wraps up at the end of April for most of them."

"That reminds me, can you connect with the three who were here last year—see if they're coming back?"

"I'll do it in the morning," said Nora. "Did you get the name of the band?"

"Yes. I'll connect with them tomorrow, too."

They passed a drive-through restaurant. "Do you want something to eat?" said Eugene.

"Sounds good."

He did a U-turn, pulled up to the restaurant, and ordered, rousing Duke from his nap in time for him to bark at the woman handing them their food. They drove home in companionable silence, munching on their burgers, until Nora and Duke fell asleep and filled the little car with their snorts and snuffles.

Eugene smiled as he drove. He could get used to these two if he wasn't careful.

CHAPTER 20

They listened to Sandy's message on the answering machine when they got to the store the next morning. Sandy would be out of town for a few weeks, and she had told Jock. She was sorry to leave them in the lurch, but she had confidence they would be just fine.

"Great," said Nora. "How are we supposed to help get them back together if she's out of town?"

"She has to come back sometime. I'll ask around in a day or two to see if anyone knows where she went. Maybe her sister's place in Santa Monica. That's where I'd go if it were me."

"Well, with any luck she's the sort of sister that gets on one's nerves in a couple of days, and Sandy will cut the trip short," said Nora. "Meanwhile, we have some work. I've found a great program for keeping track of stock that I'd like to put in place. It will take about a week, but business is slow this month according to the Jock's records, so I thought I'd get started. Any objections?"

"Not one," said Eugene, pulling Jock's stock book from the shelf under the counter. "Here you go. I'll be right out here, dusting, organizing…"

"Don't forget to call that band. And if you get bored, you could probably practice out here. It may bring in people who want to listen."

"That's a great idea. It'll advertise the band too. I'll be playing Eagles tunes."

"You'll be great, Gene. I'm so glad you're getting this opportunity after all this time."

"Thanks, Nora," he called to her retreating back. He picked up the phone and made the call to the band's agent to confirm the show.

"Glad you called, Gene," said Marilu. "I was wondering if we still had this gig. And it's great timing. The band will need you then. The guy who's filling in is expecting a baby, and if he plays past June, he'll be heading for a divorce."

"Well, we wouldn't want that." Gene laughed. "And it's perfect for my timing as well."

"We're fully booked until the end of the summer. I hope you're up to it."

"Absolutely." He would have to kick up his practice and let the construction company know he wouldn't be there this year after all. Playing music all day instead of hammering nails sounded like heaven.

Two days later, Eugene was helping one of the local music teachers pick out some books, and Nora was sitting at the counter, reviewing the stock and trying to track down their latest order. Jock had sent it in over three months earlier but, according to the supplier, they were having supply chain issues. Now that she had a good accounting of the stock, she had found that to be the case with several other items as well: Jock had ordered them, but they hadn't arrived. Or he hadn't followed up.

Eugene had just rung up the sale and bid the customer farewell when the door opened again, and Duke barked with glee. "Mom? I was just going to call you!" Nora hopped up and ran around the counter to hug her mother. "What are you doing here early? Where's Dad?"

"Why were you going to call me? Has something gone wrong with Jock?"

"No. I just wanted the name of your supplier for guitar strings."

"Call Rob. He found someone local. We've been having a hard time getting things the past few months, too."

"Thanks. I will. Now, why are you here so early?"

"Sandy called. Told me she had to visit her sister and that you and Eugene would need help."

Eugene raised his eyebrows with a knowing look, and Nora smiled. "Did she say how long she'd be away? She left rather suddenly."

"No. A few weeks at least. But she said I could stay at her condo and that Jock could stay in the spare room for a few days until Eugene finds him a more permanent solution."

"Glad she's giving us some breathing room. I'm having trouble finding a place to rent, but I have my feelers out. There's a bungalow a few blocks up that comes up mid-May."

"And Dad?"

"Your father will fly down in a couple of weeks. His business trip has been extended. He's set up a few more meetings with clients."

"And where is he this month?"

"South America."

"Don't you ever want to just travel with him?"

"I plan to—once I'm assured you and your brother are settled."

"Mom, you don't need to worry about us. We're grown-ups."

"I realize that, but Rob needs help. Being a single parent isn't easy. And you, well, I feel bad that I haven't been more available to help you. So after my trip I'll come back, make sure Jock has things back to normal and, once your divorce is final, help you pack up."

"Pack up?"

"You don't plan to stay in Seattle, do you?"

"No, I don't think so, but…"

"Then you're coming home. You can help Rob with the store until you get your accounting business up and running. We have room at the house."

"At the house? I'm not moving to your house."

"Well, you can live in the cabin out by the lake if you prefer."

"No."

"Why not? You don't have plans. You've been living in a dark basement for a year. Why would you even want to stay down here?"

"Why are you so worried about me now? I've been on my own for nearly a year."

"I told you. I've been helping Rob look after Zack and the store. Rob's needed me. I'm sorry if you feel I wasn't there for you, but…"

The door to the store opened then, and a group of young women walked in.

"Hi, Eugene. We're here for our lesson," said the one in the lead.

"Hello, there. Yes, right on time. Let's go to the lesson room and start, shall we?" Eugene motioned for the women to walk ahead of him down the hall and followed behind, giving Nora a small smile of commiseration as he passed.

"Mom, let's not speak about this right now, okay? I have a store to look after, and you need to get yourself settled in Sandy's place. Maybe drive down to see how Jock is doing?"

"I'm sorry," said her mother. "I didn't want things to start out this way. I just want you to be safe."

"I know. But I'm not a child anymore."

"You're my child. You'll always be my child."

"I realize that, Mom, but I'm also a grown woman, and I need to figure out my life for myself."

Her mom looked at her for a moment, then nodded. "Yes, you're right. Let's talk about this later. I've been traveling all day. If you give me Sandy's key, I'll go there first."

"Sandy's key?"

"She left a set in the till."

"Oh, I wondered what those were for." Nora walked around to the till and opened it, reaching into the back of the tray and pulling out a key on a keyring. She handed it to her mother. "I'll see you later, okay? Maybe you could come around for dinner."

"I think today I'll drive over and see my brother. I have a friend in Santa Barbara I haven't seen in years. I'll be back in a day or two."

"Friend? You never mentioned a friend in Santa Barbara."

"I had a life before you were born, dear." Then she squeezed Nora's arm, bent to pat

Duke on the head, and exited the same way she'd come in, taking the whirlwind she had created with her.

"Well, boy, I guess it's just you and me again." A high-pitched giggle came from the back room, and a voice said, "Oh, Eugene, you're so funny."

She shook her head and tried to focus on the task in front of her, but her mother's words kept returning. Should she move home? The cabin could be a pleasant place to live. She could probably buy her parents out eventually, and it would be nice to be close to Rob and Zack. Especially since she wasn't likely to have children of her own.

She tried again to focus on the computer screen, but she was too restless, so she walked around and straightened up the store, took out a duster and dusted as hard as she could. Why had her life turned out like this?

All she'd ever wanted was a career and a family of her own. Instead, she was in a virtual desert, alone. But at least here she was useful to Jock. At least here she was helping some small businesses with their taxes. At least here she was with people who cared.

She looked toward the hallway where Eugene was teaching. If only he cared about her as much as she did about him. She shook her head at her own thoughts. Eugene would leave soon. She would be alone. What she needed to do—after getting Jock's store back up and running, maybe hiring a replacement for Sandy—was to get her own life on track. And perhaps Sunshine Bay would be the place to do that.

When she had finished all the shelves, she moved over to polish the piano and guitars and soon became aware that the music coming from the back room had stopped.

"Thanks, Eugene."

"See you next week."

"That was great!"

The back door opened and closed before she heard steps approaching. Duke jumped and ran toward Eugene, yapping with excitement.

"I could get used to this," said Eugene, bending over to pat the little dog on the head and give him a treat from his pocket.

"To what? Group music lessons?"

"What?" Then he glanced behind him and waved his hand. "Not them. I meant Duke. He's always happy to see his people. I like being one of his people."

"And if you keep giving him so many treats, you will become his very favorite person."

Eugene laughed and patted Duke again, then stood up and looked around the room. "Where's Doris?"

"She's gone to put her stuff at Sandy's. Then she's driving into Santa Barbara to see Jock and to visit an old friend. Though who, I'm not sure."

"It must be nice to have her visit. And she's offered to help you move."

"If I move home."

"And? Are you planning to move home?"

"I don't know, Geno. Maybe I'd be better off there. It's not like I have a lot of reasons to stay here."

"You could help Jock. He's going to need it for at least six months, especially if Sandy doesn't come round."

"I could. Yes. But maybe my mother's right. Maybe I should go home, start my life again. Make some new friends. I need a place to belong, Eugene. A place with friends. A place to call home. Being in limbo isn't working for me."

"But…" he said, then stopped before he finished his thought.

"But?"

"Nothing. I've got to go see Aaron about something. I'll see you later."

~

Eugene walked toward the inn, knowing he had no reason to see Aaron. But he needed to put distance between him and Nora. To give himself space to understand his tangled feelings.

The idea of her leaving disturbed him, and he didn't know why. He had no hold on her. And besides, he was leaving soon too. Traveling again. Away from

Jock and Making Sweet Music, away from Cataluma and old friends he had been reconnecting with, and away from Nora.

He walked past the inn and down to a path along the river, picking up a rock and throwing it into the water. Why did this upset him so much? He had traveled for years. And he had looked forward to playing in the band for months.

He stooped to pick up another rock and aimed it at a small piece of wood floating past him. He missed, so he picked up a couple more stones to try again.

It wasn't like he had anything to offer Nora. He didn't have a house or even a car. He could only offer her what he had been offering for the past few weeks: support, music, and love.

He flung the last rock, which hit the wood with a crack. Love.

He loved her. He could offer her love, and what she said she wanted most: family. Belonging. But would she be willing to stay with him? To trust that he could be here for her? Stay with her?

Could she see that they belonged together, too?

Or would she leave, just like all the others had done?

He ought to leave before he was in too deep again, but even as he thought it, he knew he was already in too deep.

He loved her. He felt more comfortable with her than he'd felt in years. She was home to him. He turned on his heel and nearly ran back to the store. He didn't want to be away from her a moment longer. He wanted to fight to keep Nora in his life.

But how would he do that? And would she feel the same way?

Nora and Eugene settled into a routine over the next few weeks. Nora looked after the books and stock and taught the children after school. Eugene watched the store, taught many of the intermediate students, and organized advanced lessons with teachers from outside Cataluma who used the store as their base. Near the end of May, two students, Shan and Colten, returned from college to take on the development of the summer programs, pick up the slack at the store, and allow Eugene time to practice for the tribute band.

At night Nora and Gene took turns cooking and visiting Jock, who was now staying at Sandy's house with Doris and who seemed to improve by the day, though he was less himself than he had been in hospital. That worried Eugene. It wasn't like Jock to be withdrawn.

~

"What do you suppose is wrong with him?" asked Eugene one evening when he and Nora had returned from a visit.

"Not sure," said Nora, handing him a coffee and sitting across from him at the table. "It could be a few things."

"Like?"

"Well, for one, it could be too much time with my mother. Doris can be a bit much if you aren't used to her, and she's been arranging things for him ever since he got out of the hospital, as though he's still her baby brother and incapable of doing things for himself."

"Her help has been great, though. She moved him into that house, made sure he had everything he needs."

"Though it could get on his nerves. Mom is always managing things, deciding when and what he eats, when he gets up, when he exercises. I know she means well, but she can be a drill sergeant. I imagine he's looking forward to when she leaves on her cruise next week."

"That could be it," said Eugene. "But normally he would at least fight back. It's like he's given up."

"You're right. It's probably more to do with Sandy leaving. Have you heard from her at all? Do you know anyone who has?"

"Not a peep. Though I wonder if your Mom might know. She was the last person to speak to her, after all. Could you ask her? She's bringing Jock to see the store tomorrow. I'll keep him busy while you take her aside to find out more."

"I could do that, but…"

"But?"

Tears formed in her eyes. "I've been avoiding being alone with my mother since she arrived. With her focusing her energy on Jock, it's given me a break."

"You're afraid she'll start talking to you about going home."

"Yes, and…"

"And? What's wrong, Nora? Has something happened?" He watched a range of emotions play across her face, and then a tear slipped down her cheek. She wiped it away quickly.

"I got a call from my lawyer yesterday. Crispin is signing the papers."

"Hey." He put down the coffee cup and crossed to the couch where she was sitting. "What's wrong? Is the settlement not what you expected?"

"It's not that," she said, turning toward him. "It's the reason he's willing to sign now. His girlfriend is pregnant. They're having a baby," she wailed. "He's found another woman to have the family I wanted. He even reversed his vasectomy for her."

"Come here," said Eugene, pulling her into his arms.

"No." She shook him off. "I'm going to go for a walk. I need to get some exercise, figure out how to face my mother knowing this. She'll just make me feel worse. She'll want to take me home and protect me from the world like I'm still ten."

"I'll talk to her instead. You spend time with Jock, and I'll take her aside." He rose then and walked to the side table to get Duke's leash. "And we can both go for a walk with the dog. I haven't had enough exercise today either."

They walked down the street and past the inn in companionable silence, Eugene holding the leash and keeping Duke at heel until Nora had her feelings under control enough to speak.

"I don't want to leave, you know. I feel at home here. I haven't felt at home for so long. Do you think Jock would let me help him run the store?"

"That's what he wants," said Eugene.

"No, Eugene. He wants you to run the store."

"That's not what Sandy said."

She stopped and looked at him. "What do you mean?"

"Sandy said he had asked her to get you interested in staying in town. That he wanted you to take over the business."

"Is that why you've been talking up the business to me?" she asked. "Are you trying to trick me into staying here and looking after your father so you can—what? Continue to pursue your music career?"

"What? No! Sandy told me that Jock wanted to set you up here. Away from Seattle."

"Well, I know that's not true. Jock told me he wanted *you* to take over the store. He was planning to retire, and he was going to ask you to stay on after the summer."

"He said nothing about it to me."

"Come on, Duke," said Nora, taking the leash out of Eugene's hand. "We're going home." She began walking back to the store, but she spun around to say, "I can't believe anything you say, Eugene. Your kindness, your help getting me involved in the community and making me feel at home. It's all been just so I would stay here and take care of Jock. While you do what you always do. Leave. Run away. You're just as bad as Crispin. I can't believe I…"

"What?"

"Nothing."

He walked after her as she retreated down the path toward what would have been, on any other occasion, an idyllic sunset walk. He grabbed her arm, spinning her back toward him. "It's not nothing. What were you going to say? You can't believe you *what*?"

She stared at him, and down at his hand on her arm. Duke stood below them, barking at the sudden tension in the air.

"What were you going to say?" he demanded, loosening his grip and moving his hand down to hers and grasping it.

"It doesn't matter," she said.

"It matters to me," he said, caressing her hand with his thumb. "It matters to me, very much."

She swallowed, and Duke gave up barking to sit on his haunches and stare up at the two, looking from one to the other until he couldn't stand the silence any longer and barked again.

"It seems to matter to him as well," said Eugene, nodding to the dog and taking a step closer. "Let me see if I can help you."

"How?"

"Well, if I were to finish that sentence, I might say, I can't believe how much I've enjoyed spending time with you."

"I've enjoyed spending time with you too," she said, "but…"

He closed the gap further, and the rest of her sentence drifted away.

"I might say I can't believe you've come to mean so much to me in such a short time, and I might ask if you agree."

"Yes," she whispered.

He came one step closer, and she didn't turn away, just looked up at him with those deep, expressive eyes of hers. "Or I would say I can't believe I fell in love with you so quickly, or how fast you've become so damned important to me. So important that I would do anything to keep you in my life."

"You love me?" she whispered.

"I do," he said, stepping forward again, closing the gap completely.

"Oh," she said, looking up into his eyes.

Duke barked again and nudged her on the leg. "Oh," she said again, looking down at the dog, then back up at Eugene. "I love you too."

Then he pulled her to him and kissed her deeply, setting Duke off again. The little dog barked and ran around them, his lead tangled around their legs. They ignored him as long as they could. Finally, she broke the kiss. "We just need to…" She looked down at their legs, and he laughed.

"It looks like even Duke thinks we belong together."

Eugene disentangled them then pushed the dog behind him and kissed her again. "Let's go home, shall we?"

"Yes, let's."

An hour later, Nora was leaning against Eugene on the couch. "What are we going to tell Jock?

"That we're together," he said, kissing the tip of her nose.

"And the store?"

"Well," he said slowly, "we'll have to convince him we can do it together. The idea of leaving… It doesn't bear thinking about."

"And your music? The band?"

"I'll help them out until they can find a replacement."

"But won't you miss the road?"

"No. I don't want to go back to my solo life. I find driving around in the Mini with a roof, and you two, to be much more preferable."

"Even though your legs get cramped?"

"Even then. Yes."

They kissed again.

"Oh, no," she said.

"What now?"

"What am I going to tell my mother?"

"We'll find a way. She'll be fine if she knows you're happy."

"Yes, I'm sure you're right."

CHAPTER 22

They didn't have to wait long to find out their family's opinion because Jock came into the store the next morning.

"Hi. Uncle Jock. How are you doing?"

"He's getting much better," Nora's mother said, and Jock stared at the ceiling.

"I see you got the guitars hung all right," he said to Eugene. "It looks just like I thought it would."

"Glad to hear," said Eugene. "What do you think of this?" he asked, pulling his father over to the other side of the room to show him a display he had built to show off their book collection.

"It looks good, Gene. Thanks for all your work on this. It feels like a whole new store. You two have done a great job."

Eugene waited until Nora took her mother to the back to get some tea then faced him. "Now tell me. How are you really doing, Dad?"

"Been working hard," said Jock, smiling wanly. "I barely need the cane when I'm walking around the house."

"Almost time to come back to work, then?"

"I suppose so." He didn't sound convinced, nor enthusiastic.

"Starting next week, Nora will need the help. I'm traveling for the next couple months until the band can find a replacement for me."

"A replacement? Does that mean you'll go back to snowboarding?"

"No. It means I'll come back to live here—once I find a place, that is. And if you'll have me."

"You'll help me look after the store after Nora leaves?" Jock smiled for the first time in weeks, reinforcing Eugene's faith in his decision.

"No. Not exactly. Nora won't be leaving."

"She won't?"

"No. Nora and I… We are…" He watched Jock's face carefully as he tried to form the words.

"You mean Sandy was right?" asked Jock.

"About what?"

"That there's something between you and Nora. She always said you two belonged together. She was right, wasn't she? She even had me trick Nora into talking you into staying, while she got you—"

"To trick Nora into staying," finished Eugene. "Nora was right. No wonder she felt she was being manipulated. She thought it was me."

"Don't be mad. Sandy was just trying to help. She doesn't have a mean bone in her body." He looked sad.

"I'm not mad. I just wish I had figured it out earlier. I would rather have just talked to Nora about it. Laid things out on the table. I don't like playing games. Especially with people I love."

"So that's the way of it, then?" said Jock. "You love her."

"Yes. And she feels the same way."

"Well, congratulations, son. I'm pleased for you. For her. For the both of you."

"I thought you'd be upset."

"If I thought it was a dalliance, I would be. But you and Nora are grown-ups. You know what you're doing."

"Thanks, Dad. It feels good to have your support."

"I just wish I could tell Sandy she was right. But I don't know where to even start looking for her. I just have to wait for her to come home and hope she speaks to me then."

"I'll help where I can."

"Thanks, Gene. I might need it." He nodded at Nora and Doris, who had just come into the room. "Have you told Doris about you two?"

"Not yet," said Eugene.

"Oh, boy," said Jock. "Well, I recommend getting it over with as soon as you can. She's leaving the day after tomorrow."

"Really?"

Jock grinned ear to ear. "Really. I love my sister, but it will be nice to see her on her way to her next project."

Eugene laughed out loud, and the two women turned toward them.

"What are you two talking about?" asked Doris. "What did you say to make my brother smile?"

"Eugene was just sharing great news with me," said Jock, turning to Eugene with a grin and only a hint of apology in his eyes. *You rat*, thought Eugene. *You'll throw anyone under the bus to get a break from Doris's machinations.*

"What kind of news is that?" asked Doris, throwing a wary look at Nora.

Nora stood tall and walked over to stand beside Eugene. "We've got something to tell you."

"What?" Doris asked.

"Jock has been thinking of selling," Eugene began, "but Nora and I have another idea we think will work."

"What's that?" Doris asked. "Don't keep me in suspense."

"We'd like to run the place ourselves," said Nora. "With Jock as well, until he's ready to sell."

"As partners?" asked Doris.

"Yes," said Eugene and Nora together.

"And what about your accounting business?"

"I can run a small one here and help a few businesses with their books. I already have five clients, and that's just been through word of mouth over the last month. I'm holding a talk at the library next week. I expect to pick up one or two there as well."

"And she does a great job," said Jock. "I got a refund this year. That's the first time in years."

Nora grinned. "I'm glad you approve, Uncle Jock. Does that mean I'm hired for next year too?" she joked, noticing her mother's frown and trying to keep the mood light. Her mother did not look pleased.

"And you? You're going to give up the band?" said Doris to Eugene.

"I'll travel for the next two months, but I've asked them to find a replacement after that."

"And what about your need to play in a band? Surely you will miss it."

"I can play locally. At the festival, the local pub. Nora and I have been playing some jazz together, and we're having a blast." He grasped Nora's hand and held on. They may as well plunge right in.

Doris looked at their clasped hands and appeared, for a moment, to get the wind knocked out of her. But a moment later she gathered her energy, took a deep breath, and turned toward Nora.

"A word in private, Honoria," she said, walking toward the back office.

Nora looked at Eugene, who nodded encouragement. Then she followed her mother like a chastened schoolgirl. *Uh-oh,* thought Eugene. When a mother used your full name, it never boded well.

CHAPTER 23

Her mother led the way into the office and spun toward Nora when they got inside.

"Close the door."

Nora closed the door and stood against it as her mother's anger emanated from the other side of the room.

"You can't do this, Nora."

"Why not?"

"He'll break your heart. You're vulnerable. Don't fall for the first man who comes along."

"He isn't the first."

That knocked the wind out of her sails again, but she was soon back. Fully primed. "He has a lousy track record. He's gone through more women than I have socks."

"It's okay. So has Crispin. But I trust Geno. He wouldn't hurt me. Besides, he's usually the dump-ee, not the one who leaves."

"He'll travel. Leave you behind."

"Like Dad, you mean?"

"Yes. You'll be left running the store. He'll be traveling with the band. He won't come back, Nora."

"Of course he will," said Nora. "He said he would only help them out until they found a replacement. Eugene is a man of his word. I trust him."

"That's what he says now, but—"

"Mom. I don't think this is about me. I think this is about Dad. And you. If you don't have me to worry about, what does that mean for you? I think you're scared you might have to do things you're always putting off."

Her mother charged on without listening. "What about children? He won't want them."

"Then I won't be any worse off than I am now. He wants me. Crispin never did."

"You just needed to…"

"To what, Mom? Work harder at holding it together? Crispin never loved me enough. Do you know he reversed his vasectomy for his girlfriend? The vasectomy he never even told me about until I had wasted money on fertility testing?"

"What?" Doris's face fell, and tears formed in her eyes.

"He was selfish. He never wanted me."

"Oh, honey. Why didn't you tell me?"

"I didn't want you to pity me."

"I wouldn't have pitied you."

"Here, I have a home. I have Jock and, if they can get it together, Sandy. And I have Eugene."

"Crispin was a selfish man. I had no idea. But what makes you think Eugene will be better? Mark my words, Honoria. He'll leave you behind to travel."

"Then maybe I'll go with him."

"Until when? Until you're fifty, sixty? Then what?"

"Mother. I don't think it will come to that. But I love him. He loves me. And wherever we are will feel like home."

"Until it's not."

"Mom, is this about me or you? Is everything okay with Dad?"

Her mother's face crumpled then. "We aren't going on a cruise. He's at a conference in San Diego."

"Why aren't you there with him?"

"He always asks me to join him, but…"

"But until now you haven't."

"What if he doesn't want me? What if he only says it out of habit?"

"Mom, what if he says it out of love? Dad adores you. He'll be thrilled."

"I hope you're right, because you two don't need me. Rob has the store well in hand. I don't know what I'm going to do next."

"Mom, you have money, health, and Dad. Rob and I are always in your corner. The way I see it, you can do anything you want now. All you need to do is figure out what that is."

Doris sat down hard on the chair behind the desk and put her head in her hands. Then she looked up again at Nora. "You know, you're right. I have time to do all the things I haven't done."

"Exactly." Then, noticing the gleam in her mother's eye, she asked warily, "What do you think you'd like to try first?"

"Trainspotting."

"Trainspotting?"

"It's how I met your father."

"I thought you met him because you were playing together in a band at university."

"We did. But the first time I saw your father was when we were both standing on an overhead bridge outside Fort Langley, taking pictures of trains."

"Really?"

"Yes. And he still does it whenever he travels near a rail line."

"That's why he sends you all those pictures of trains?"

"Yes."

"Well, there you have it. Every time he takes a picture of a train, he's thinking about you. Probably wishing you were with him."

"You think?"

"I know."

"Thank you, Honoria."

"Now, when is your plane to San Diego?"

"I fly the day after tomorrow from Santa Barbara."

"Dad will be thrilled."

"I hope so. But I need your help with something before I go. Can you get away for a few hours? Maybe leave Duke with Eugene?"

"I could ask him. What's this about?"

"It's about Sandy and my thick-headed brother."

"Do you even know where she is? She was angry enough to go to her sister's house."

"She's back," said Doris. "She swore me to secrecy at first, but a few people in town have spotted her. She's been home for nearly three weeks. I met her in Santa Barbara after I visited Jock the first day I was here."

"I thought she went to see her sister. What was she doing in Santa Barbara?"

"She wanted to be close to Jock."

"Each is as bad as the other."

"I know. Will you help?"

"What can we do?"

"Well, right now she's at home," Doris explained. "She's been downsizing her house. Packing things up. She wants to put it on the market. She says she can't stay."

"Is that why Jock's sad?"

"He doesn't know. He hasn't been out except to walk around the block and get used to his new hip. He's been working hard on his physio. He wants to be ready for when she comes back."

"Is that why he's so tired?"

"Yes. And grumpy. I'm not sure what hurts more: his hip or his heart."

"What can I do to help?"

"Come with me to visit her. I have a plan."

CHAPTER 24

"Hi, Sandy," said Doris, as she and Nora stepped into the condominium. "We're here to help you."

"Oh, you didn't need to do that," said Sandy, smiling hard, though it was clear she hadn't been smiling before they came. Her eyes were bloodshot, and she looked thinner than she had a month earlier.

"How are you?" Doris asked, hugging her. Nora looked around at the piles of paper, clothes, and other belongings. There were a few boxes packed in the corner, but it didn't look like she was making any headway. For a woman who always seemed so organized, it wasn't like her.

"Where would you like us to start?" asked Doris. "Which room are you working on today?"

Sandy looked from Doris to Nora and back to Doris. "Oh, Doris, I thought I could do it. I thought I could pack up, leave, go south to be nearer my sister, but…"

"But you'd be leaving your home?" asked Doris gently.

"Yes," she choked out. "It was hard enough to move from my old house to this place after Blake died." Her sobs got louder. "What was I thinking?"

"Come here. Sit down. Nora, go make us some tea."

Nora retreated to the kitchen, filled the kettle with water, and found three cups and a tray to put them on. When she felt like she'd wasted enough time and given the two women their privacy enough for Sandy to calm down, she returned to the living room to ask if they wanted cream and sugar. She found Sandy laughing.

"Are you serious? He's actually walking on his own?"

"He's using a walker if we go very far, and a cane around the house, but he's working hard. Improving."

"And Nora, you've decided to stay and help Jock with the store?"

"Yes, and we've updated the systems in his absence. He hasn't complained."

"Even the stock?"

"Uh-huh." Nora left and came back to hand around mugs of tea. She sat down to join them and listened in wonder at how well her mother steered Sandy in the direction she wanted her to go.

"What about Gene? What's he doing?"

Her mother turned toward her, and Nora felt herself blushing under their collective gaze. "He's staying too," said Nora. "He and I are—"

"Together?" squealed Sandy." I knew it. I told Jock."

"What did you tell Jock?" Nora asked, wary that they had been discussing her personal life behind her back. After all of Crispin's betrayals, it was still hard to trust. Hard to believe that people had her best interests at heart.

Sandy sat back a bit and said hesitantly, "Just that the two of you belonged together. I remember how you used to follow him around when you were a teenager. You two have chemistry, Nora. Chemistry and compatibility. A brilliant combination. That's why we did what we did."

"And what exactly did you and Jock do?"

"I told him I would get Eugene to talk you into staying, and he got you to talk Eugene into staying. That way, we could finally retire."

"Well, that part of your plan worked. So why don't you retire with Jock?"

"Jock isn't interested in that with me. "

Nora looked at Doris and then shook her head. "That is bull crap," said Nora.

"He's been spending time with that traitor, Virginia!"

"Sandy, I'm going to tell you this, but if you ever tell Jock, I will deny it."

"Tell me what?"

"He's been teaching Virginia to sing. That note you saw—the envelope on his table—it was a check. Not a love note."

"Why would she need singing lessons?" scoffed Sandy. "I'm sorry, but you're wrong, Nora."

"Sandy, why do you think Jock has been working so hard to get better? He wants to be good enough for *you*. Not Virginia." Nora waved her hand behind her toward city hall then pointed as Sandy. "You."

"What about him going to Canada?"

"He's not coming north," said Doris. "Except to visit for Christmas, maybe. But my brother has no intention of leaving. Not now that Eugene and Nora are taking over the store."

Sandy looked doubtful, but hope sparked in her eyes. "You really think he'll stay?"

"Sandy, that man has been miserable," said Doris. "And he has been trying my patience to where I am nearly at the end of my rope."

"He does get crabby when he doesn't get what he wants," said Sandy. "And he hates sitting around."

"He's even talking about traveling."

"Traveling?"

"It's his turn, he says. As soon as Eugene gets back from his brief tour."

"So Eugene is still going with the band?"

"Until they can find a replacement, yes."

"And how do you feel about that, Nora?" asked Sandy.

"Nora is fine with it," answered Doris. "Nora is fine no matter what happens with Eugene. And I couldn't be prouder of her."

"Thanks, Mom," said Nora, wishing she had recorded those words. She wanted to tell Rob about this little conversation, but her brother would never believe it.

"Are we ready?" Nora asked the children the next day. "We have guests coming to listen to how hard you've all been practicing."

The children sat up in their chairs and raised their instruments in readiness for Nora's signal.

"We're going to start with a warm-up until they get here so we are ready. Then we'll play our first piece." She led the band through their scales and then some harmonies, pleased with the sound they were making. The children were all under ten, and some had only been playing for a few months, but they had been working hard and sounded quite good already. In a month, when they played at the festival, she felt sure they would be completely prepared.

As they were finishing their warm-up, the door opened, and Doris came in with Sandy. They sat on chairs at the front of the room, and Nora said, "Okay, everyone, let's start with our medley." And they were off, playing a series of children's songs that included "Farmer in the Dell" and "Bingo." When they were done, Nora turned around to bow in response to Sandy's enthusiastic applause.

"That was wonderful," said Sandy. "You've all been working so hard, I can tell," she praised.

"Would you like to hear another one?" asked Nora.

"They have two prepared?"

"Yes," said Eugene, who had slipped into the room to. "This is a talented group," he added, earning smiles from all eighteen of the children.

"I would love to hear more," said Sandy, and Nora the children moved on to the next song, a lovely rendition of "Row, Row, Row Your Boat" and "The Streets of Laredo."

When they were done, Sandy was standing and clapping with enthusiasm. "Bravo," she said. "What a lovely show."

"And next week we will start on 'Scarborough Fair,'" said Nora. "By the time we play at the festival, we will have a full fifteen minutes."

"Thank you all for letting me sit in on your practice," said Sandy.

"You're welcome, Sandy," the children said in a chorus. Nora watched Sandy leave with Eugene, but her mother remained.

"I want to hear a replay," said Doris, smiling at the children. Nora picked up the baton, the children raised their instruments, and after she counted out the tempo, they began all over again. The music, clear and in harmony, filled the room, and Nora moved her hands to the beat she wanted them to follow. For the first time since she'd heard of Crispin's betrayal, she was glad he'd done it. Because since he'd been gone, she'd been able to bring music back into her life.

CHAPTER 26

"I hope you like what we've done with the place," said Eugene. "We've got more plans for next year, though, like painting the walls in the class-room in a calmer color and starting a small jazz band."

"I can't wait to see it," said Sandy, fol-lowing Eugene to the front of the store. They paused at the office.

"Nora has been mostly responsible for this. I think it was so she could work in here comfortably." He laughed.

"Oh, my," said Sandy as she looked around the room. "You'd never know this was the same room."

"I installed a few shelves," said Eugene, pointing at the far wall. "And Nora found some containers and banker's boxes. I think it turned out well."

"I agree. You two have certainly put your all into this. I knew you could do it."

"Thanks for the vote of confidence, Sandy. It means a lot. Now come."

She followed him to the front of the store and glanced around at some of the changes they had made. "More shelves. These are lovely," she said, running her hand over the smooth wood surface. "And I love the display." She pointed up at the guitars.

"They have done a great job, haven't they?" A gruff voice came from behind the counter where Jock had been sitting, slightly out of sight.

"Oh!" Sandy jumped. "You scared the Dickens out of me."

"I'm sorry," said Jock, standing and walking carefully around the counter toward her. He left his cane behind. When he got to her, he said again, "I'm sorry for everything."

Eugene stepped back and made his way to the counter, leaving them as much privacy as he could.

"Can you forgive me?" Jock was saying.

"Perhaps," said Sandy.

"I was completely lost when you left. I never want to lose you again. You make my life whole, Sandy."

"Oh, Jock!" said Sandy. "Do you mean it?"

"Come here," he said, drawing her toward the back room. "We have a lot of lost time to make up for."

"Oh, Jock!"

Eugene smiled as they disappeared behind the curtain to the back room. Now he could go off on his trip knowing all was right with his family. He just wished he didn't have to go for such a long time.

"Well, that worked out well," said Doris, who was coming in through the curtain where the couple had disappeared only a few moments earlier.

Eugene chuckled. "Yes, I'm happy to see Dad smiling again. He was becoming impossible."

"Try living with that for three weeks," said Doris.

"So are you off now?" asked Eugene.

"I am," said Doris. "I'm parked out back, and I'll say goodbye to Nora in a few minutes. I just wanted to stop by and see you first."

Eugene braced himself. He never knew what to expect with Doris.

"I wanted to thank you," she said. "For helping my Nora find happiness again. She's done wonders with those children and seems to really enjoy teaching music."

"She is wonderful with them," said Eugene. "They all want to work hard for her."

"And for you too, I think. I can see you two make a good team and you have my blessing—not that you need it."

"Thank you, Doris. I appreciate that."

"Just don't break her heart. I don't know if I can watch her go through that again. "

"I won't," said Eugene. "Not without breaking my own."

"Well, I'm off. Give me a hug, young man." And she pulled him in for a big bear hug that told Eugene he had Doris on his side.

A formidable ally, yes. But not, he was sure, someone he ever wanted to cross.

EPILOGUE

"Are you ready?" Nora asked the children, who were sitting on the stage of the bandstand in the center of the festival grounds.

"They are," said Sandy from beside her. She'd been helping them set up their music stands and ensuring their instruments were ready to go.

"Have you seen Eugene yet?" Nora asked under her breath. "I thought he'd be here today."

"He'll be here. If not today, he'll definitely be here by tomorrow morning. They play tomorrow night."

"You're right, of course," said Nora, tamping down her concern. She hadn't heard from him for three days, which wasn't like him. It wasn't like him at all.

"He'll get here. Meanwhile, focus on what you need to do. The kids are ready."

"And Duke?"

"He's tied up just over there." Sandy pointed to the little dog at the bottom of the stairs. "I'll get him right now and make sure he has water. You focus on the concert."

"Okay." Nora tapped her baton on the music stand, and all the children turned their attention toward her. She raised the baton, and the children raised their instruments in unison, ready to play.

"One, two, three, four," Nora counted out. Then she signaled for the trumpets to begin. As the music rose around her, she smiled, happy that the band was doing so well. But in the back of her mind she wondered where Eugene was, and when she would see him again.

Fifteen minutes later, the children rose, bowed, and filed off the stage to put their instruments away. The children from the junior high school band filed on to take their place. Nora went around to the back of the stage to congratulate the children and chat with the proud parents helping their children put away their instruments. She agreed that the kids had sounded fantastic. Several parents said they would be over to the store to sign up for the summer camp, and she basked for a moment in the praise. It had been hard work motivating the children to practice every day but, in the end, they had played well. It was worth it.

She looked forward to the summer program, when she could introduce them to more challenging material, but meanwhile she needed to get a drink of water and find Duke and Sandy.

As Nora walked back to the front of the stage, she heard a guitar being tuned, but she didn't pay much attention until she recognized the melody. The first bars of "Love Will Keep Us Alive" rang out and she turned toward the stage, her heart pounding.

Eugene. He was back, and he was up on the stage playing a solo.

He sang out the first few words—about loneliness, about finding each other, about love—and she grinned wider than she ever had. He smiled back and continued to sing until he got to the end of the song. Then he came down the steps to where she stood, vibrating with the excitement of seeing her. But before she could run toward him, he held up his hand to stop her. Instead, he approached her, leaned his guitar against a nearby chair, looked into her eyes, and sank to one knee.

"What are you doing?" she asked.

"When you know, you know," he said. "And when you find someone you don't want to let go of, you ask her to stay. Stay with me, Nora. Be my wife."

"Say yes!" a chorus of voices shouted from around the festival grounds.

"Say yes," said Sandy, as she made her way back to the stage with Duke.

Duke tore himself free of Sandy's grip and raced across the field, his leash trailing behind him. He jumped into Eugene's arms, licking at his face and squeaking in delight.

"Well, how can I say no after a display like that?" asked Nora. "Duke always did have a good sense of people."

"Is that a yes, then?" asked Eugene, grinning up at her while Sandy recaptured Duke.

"Of course it's a yes," said Nora, accepting the ring Eugene was slipping onto her finger. She held it out to look at it and then grabbed his hands and pulled him to his feet. "Come here, you," she said. And, to the delight of Sandy, Jock, the crowd, and especially Duke, she kissed him soundly.

"I've missed you," said Nora.

"I'm back for good," he said. "Today is my last show with the band. I helped them find a replacement."

"Well, I'm glad you are back because Sandy and Jock are leaving in a week. They're joining my parents on a cruise."

Eugene chuckled and kissed her again. "It's about time Jock stepped up and took Sandy on a vacation. Good for him."

"What do you want to do now?" she asked. "Do you want to go home, put your things away?"

"Darlin'," said Eugene, "when I'm with you, I am home."

And he kissed her again, setting Duke to barking in delight.

Love *Something of Note*? Check out *Making Sweet Music*, the story of Nora's brother Robert.

Making Sweet Music is part of the Shops at Sunshine Bay series.

ABOUT THE AUTHOR

Jeanine Lauren is a USA Today bestselling author who writes stories about friendship, love and second chances in the second half of life, because let's face it, the second half is the most interesting.

To find out when Jeanine's next books are coming out, head over to her website at jeaninelauren.com and join her mailing list.

Jeanine lives in the lower mainland of British Columbia, Canada not far from the fictional town of Sunshine Bay where most of her characters live.

www.ingramcontent.com/pod-product-compliance
Lightning Source LLC
Chambersburg PA
CBHW061653190726
48289CB00006B/1859